HEARTWOOD

by Mary E. Burns

Illustrated by Peggy Grinvalsky

MANITOWISH RIVER PRESS
Mercer, Wisconsin

HEARTWOOD

Copyright © 2003 by Mary E. Burns. All rights reserved. Except for short excerpts for review purposes, no part of this book may be reproduced or transmitted in any form by any means, electronic or mechanical, without permission in writing from the publisher.

Printed in the United States on 30% recycled paper.

Illustrations: Peggy Grinvalsky
Cover illustration: Peggy Grinvalsky
Book design: Katie Miller
Cover design: Katie Miller

Publisher's Cataloging in Publication Data
Burns, Mary E.
Heartwood
   Written by Mary E. Burns; illustrated by Peggy Grinvalsky
   ISBN 0-9656763-4-x (softcover)

Summary: Kelly and her grandfather journey through portals of time to bring the spirit of the white pines into the future.
   1. Fantasy – Juvenile Fiction.
   2. Natural History - Juvenile Fiction.
   3. Great Lakes Region - Juvenile Fiction.

Library of Congress Catalog Card Number: 2003107352

Printed in the United States of America
10 9 8 7 6 5 4 3 2 1

Published by: Manitowish River Press
             4245N Hwy. 47
             Mercer, WI 54547
             Phone: (715) 476-2828
             Fax: (715) 476-2818
             E-mail: manitowish@centurytel.net
             Web site: www.manitowish.com

This book is dedicated to my husband John and to our daughters, Eowyn and Callie

Acknowledgments

Many thanks to my writers' group who gave me wonderful encouragement and feedback, with special thanks to Greg Linder. My thanks to Peggy Grinvalsky, whose artwork embodies the spirit of this book; it is a perfect match. Thank you to Katie Miller for her infectious enthusiasm and sense of design. Thanks to my family who got me out in the forests as a child, especially my sister who always set up camp with me under Grandpa's "big pines." Thank you, John and Callie, for keeping the heartlight of this book lit.

Chapter 1
The Dreams

"Help! Help!" someone was calling from the trees.

"Help me!" the cry came again.

Kelly strained her eyes but couldn't see anyone. "Where are you?" she called.

"Over here. Help!"

Kelly struggled on through the deep snow, grabbing onto a tree for support. She peered ahead into the twilight; soon it would be completely dark. "Help!" This time the cry was more muffled. She lunged forward, sinking to her thighs in the snow, but she pushed on, dragging her heavy, snow-laden legs through the dense white sea.

"I'm coming," she yelled. Who could be out in the forest on a night like this? A lost traveler? An injured trapper? The huge dark trunks of the pines towered over her, their shapes black and menacing in the fading light.

"Kelly!" the faint voice cried. A rasping sound ripped the air.

It must be one of the neighbors, maybe Mr. Dawson. Kelly plunged through the snow, but she slipped and sank deep into a drift. She kicked out with her feet, trying to find her balance, but she only sank deeper. The coldness was all around, in her face, in her eyes. Heavy, wet snow filled her nostrils. She gasped for breath.

"Kelly. Kelly," the low voice called.

Kelly awoke slowly as if she were swimming up through an ocean and trying to reach the surface for air. She opened her eyes. Her room was softly lit by the dawn light; even in the dimness, she could see that no one was in the room.

Kelly took a deep breath and slowly sat up in bed, frowning. This was the third night this week she had been awakened. Was there someone calling her, or was she dreaming again? All she could recall was the low quiet voice calling, "Kelly, Kelly."

Getting out of bed, she walked over to the nearest window and looked behind the folds of yellow material that hugged the wall. The curtain produced no robbers or thieves. Could it have been a dream?

Turning around, she crossed the room to the hallway door. Her hand closed over the black porcelain handle; slowly and carefully she turned the knob and inched the door open. It squeaked, and she stopped abruptly, afraid the noise might awaken someone. She poked her head through the small opening and peered up and down the dark hallway. No one was about. Quietly, Kelly closed the door and crept back into bed. The voice must have been a dream after all.

Kelly rested her hands on the windowsill and looked out. She never drew the curtains closed in the summer; she wanted every last microscopic spore of early summer air to come in. She would have slept outdoors all summer if Grandma Ann and Grandpa Evan had let her. But at their latest "summit conference," Grandma Ann claimed that certain twelve year olds could sleep outside sometimes but not every night.

The eastern sky was reddening above the black-silhouetted pines. The prospect of a sunny, northern Wisconsin day made her smile. Then she thought of her Grandma's old saying, "Red sky at morning, sailors take warning; red sky at night, sailors delight." She hoped the sailors were wrong about today. It was her first day of summer, and she intended to be out all day.

As she watched, the darkness continued to fade, and only Venus burned brilliant enough to be seen. Kelly picked up her hairbrush from the window ledge. She brushed her long black hair up into a ponytail and cinched the hair-tie tightly in place. She saw her reflection in the window, and she looked tired but excited. She was slight for her age but strong. At school she won all of the running events in her class.

The furnishings of the room were simple. Her four-poster bed was pushed headfirst against the center of the south wall. From the bed she could look across the room at the shelves that held her books. She'd arranged them by author and liked to see how one shelf was dominated by Madeline L'Engle, another by Laura Ingalls Wilder, and a third lined with folktales from around the world. The double doors that led into the guest room were in the center of the wall, directly opposite her bed.

Nestled between the two windows to the right of Kelly's bed stood a dark oak desk. The desk had belonged to her great-grandfather, and his initials, "C.O.," were etched into one of the drawers. It had a large work surface, with three drawers below, on either side of the chair. Her computer looked modern and out of place against the dark wood, but Kelly loved it. Behind the desktop rose a set of drawers and cubicles. Cubbyholes and secret compartments divided the space, with room for storing her work and all the things she collected, like feathers, stones, and small pieces of driftwood.

Wood circled the entire room; the tall planks ran from floor to ceiling. The walls and doors were paneled in golden pine, with deep brown knots. Reddish-brown patterns stood out against the lighter-colored wood. Her grandmother had told her that the lightwood grew on the outer edges of the trees, and the reddish-brown wood was formed by the center of the tree. "That is the heartwood of the tree, Kelly. It's like the soul of every tree is alive in its dark center."

Kelly often scanned the walls of her room and found animal and plant shapes in the wood grain. The deep knots in the wood always became eyes, which, she thought, watched her movements. The eyes did not frighten her as they had when she was younger. Kelly now thought of them as sad and pensive, looking out at her quietly from the flatness of the walls.

She had grown to like these shapes in her walls and even named some of her favorite ones. She'd call to them and they seemed to look at her out of their knotty eyes and smile. The pine figure she found most attractive, and yet the most puzzling, formed the double doors between her room and the guest room. Like a hooded monk, its face was hidden but for one dark, brooding eye and the tip of its hawk-like nose. At times she thought she could almost see him breathing.

Kelly watched the monk briefly and then pulled the sheet up over her head. She thought about the voice in the night. It had called her as if trying to wake her: "Kelly, Kelly."

Later that morning, Kelly sat at the base of a huge white pine. She leaned back against its dark, corky bark and let the stillness of the forest surround her. This was her favorite place to come and be alone. Such a peaceful quietness pervaded the woods here that she felt she absorbed it through her skin. The pines rose from the forest floor like towers holding up the sky or like the stone columns in the old museum in the city.

Few plants survived beneath the shady pines, making the forest look like a park. There were trails through the woods, but the forest was so open that Kelly could walk almost anywhere. The boughs filtered the sunlight through their branches, dappling the ground below with beads of light.

A chickadee called from overhead, and another answered. A red squirrel skittered about, gathering seeds. Kelly shut her eyes slowly and breathed in the resinous, piney air.

Suddenly she felt cold, as if a chill wind were blowing through the trees. Goosebumps prickled her spine. She felt heavy. The air turned icy. She shivered. Her hands felt as if they were made of marble. Frost seemed to cling to her. She was sinking down into icy depths. The coldness pressed in on her.

Her dream. She had been dreaming of the snow. Someone needed help, and she couldn't reach him or her. And now she was surrounded by the cold. The frigid air paralyzed her limbs. The heavy, suffocating cold knelt on her chest. She struggled to breathe.

"Kelly, Kelly," a voice called. "Kelly, where are you?"

She opened her eyes. The pressure on her lungs eased. The cold lessened. But she still shivered.

"Kelly!" the call came again. Kelly shook her head. She dragged herself to her feet.

"Over here, Grandpa."

The day had darkened. Morning warmth had been followed by thick black clouds and cool, steady rain. Kelly sat in her bed, a cup of hot chocolate in her hands.

Grandma pulled another blanket from the closet and laid it over the foot of the bed. Her black and gray hair coiled around her head in a smooth braid. She wore a soft, mossy-colored flannel shirt and blue jeans.

Grandpa sat in the chair by the desk. His thick white hair matched his mustache and bushy eyebrows. His eyebrows were so heavy they almost met in the center, but there was enough space for the worry-line that now creased his forehead. "What do you make of these dreams, Kelly?" he asked.

She sipped the hot chocolate. "I don't know, but they

really scare me." She leaned against the headboard. "I didn't even think I'd fallen asleep out in the woods. It was so real; I thought I was freezing." She shivered slightly. "My lungs hurt, the air was so cold."

"Well, dream or not, you were mighty cold when I found you." Grandpa watched her closely.

"I might just keep you in that bed for a week," Grandma said as she sat down on the edge of the bed. She gave Evan a wink.

"Not for a week, Grandma!" Kelly made a face. "But this bed feels pretty good right now," she admitted. "I still feel a little cold."

"By the looks of this weather it won't matter for a few days. We can lay low until June gets this rain out of its system." Grandpa looked out the window. The rain drizzled steadily against the pane. He had gone out looking for Kelly to tell her that the two of them had been cleared for camping: Grandma had decided not to go on this camping trip.

"Grandma, why aren't you going with us?" Kelly demanded.

"Unfortunately, I've got work to do." Grandma sighed. "Some rare plants have been found near Eton's planned mine site over in Eagle Creek. Jan Smithton asked if I'd come and help with the identification of these species."

"Maybe we should all volunteer to help out for a few days," Grandpa suggested.

"Yeah!" Kelly straightened up. "Then the work would get done more quickly, and we could all go camping."

"I appreciate that, but. . . ."Grandma frowned. "The work is at a critical stage, and it might take more time than we initially thought. If we can identify any of these plants as endangered—there may be a few remnant

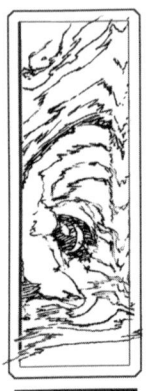 patches on the mine site itself—we might be able to slow construction down long enough to ensure that the mining is done right. We have to figure out how to protect the plant species while they figure out how to construct the mine without damaging the environment. It's a difficult balance between extraction and protection, but there must be a way to find that balance."

"Given the importance of your research, it's probably best if Kel and I tramp about on our own on this first trip." Evan rubbed his chin thoughtfully. "On the other hand, I don't know if I can put up with this girl on my own." He looked seriously at Kelly, but there was a twinkle of merriment in his blue eyes.

"Oh, Grandpa!"

Grandma laughed. "You two will be fine! This way you can get all the gear organized and ready for the summer tripping, and I'll join you on the next excursion."

"Make us do all the work, as usual," Grandpa teased.

Kelly laughed and rolled her eyes.

The wind blew harder against the windows, and a crack of thunder rumbled overhead. Kelly shuddered and Grandma pulled the blanket tighter around her, giving her a hug. "Are you all right?"

"Yeah," she answered as she glanced around her bedroom. "But I think sitting in front of the fire would help warm me up even more."

Kelly waddled downstairs with her blankets and stretched out on the couch, the wool comforter wrapped around her shoulders.

Grandma carried in a bundle of firewood and set it down next to the fireplace. She poked at the fire, shifting the logs on the grate.

Grandpa walked into the room, maps and guidebooks in hand, and stood next to the couch. "If this blasted rain ever stops, we'll go camping. But it's raining even harder now than it was earlier this afternoon. The temp's dropped again, too." He shook his head. "I don't like the feel of this weather; it doesn't feel right for June."

"You know our teachers taught us that May and June are the tornado months," Kelly said. "I thought it was the hot, sticky August days that bred tornadoes, but I guess not. It's the in-between time when it's not spring anymore and summer hasn't quite arrived that creates tornado weather."

Evan looked down at his granddaughter. "Well, I didn't say it was tornado weather; it just doesn't feel right. Now scoot over and let this old man sit down next to you." Kelly curled her legs under her, making room for him on the couch.

Grandma finished laying the new logs on the grate. She sat down in the rocker and eyed the two on the couch. "Kelly, are you still cold even with this blazing fire and a big wool blanket?"

"No, I'm not cold anymore. It just feels great to sit here." She looked into the flames as they wrapped themselves around the new logs. "When I first came to live here, you let me choose my own room. But when I picked it out, neither of you wanted me to take that one. You wanted me to move into Uncle Conor's old room. But I insisted on having my way. I was pretty little then, and you kept saying that Conor's room would be closer to yours, and it would be better for me. But that wasn't the real reason, was it? Why didn't you want me to have that bedroom?"

"Oh, there was no real reason, Kel. Evan and I just thought you'd be better off next to our room instead of way down the hall on your own." Grandma smiled at her.

"Yes," Grandpa said. "We wanted you to be safe and close to us." He patted her knee. "We didn't want you having nightmares down there on your own, without us nearby to help you."

"But I never have nightmares. Well, at least not until now. I never had them when I was little. And I've always loved that room; it feels so good. You know, even before I came to live here, when I'd just come to visit, I wanted to stay in that room. It was my favorite place in the whole house." She leaned her head on his shoulder. "I was really happy when you let me have it."

"That room holds a lot of history, just like the rest of the house," replied Grandpa. "It's a special room. Your great-grandfather Charles loved it as you do. Maybe you understand it in a way that I never could. I could never stay in it, maybe because it was my father's room, and it held too much of him for me to be comfortable there."

He stroked her hair. "Kel, you'll sleep well tonight. If you've never had nightmares before this summer, there's no reason to start now."

She woke in the night. The rain had stopped, and the moon shone cold and clear on her bed. It seemed to Kelly that the only sound was her own slow, steady breathing. There had been no sound, no calling that had awakened her. But she was wide awake. She carefully surveyed her room: Everything seemed to be in its place.

Kelly felt her chest tighten as if a heavy stone were crushing her. The stillness was closing in upon her—a smothering, cold quiet like snow drifting on top of her. She couldn't move.

A wind began to blow in the pines. Softly the boughs brushed one another and the branches whispered. The tension began to drain from her arms and legs. She somehow understood there was nothing in her room to be frightened of. Her fear had grown only in her imagination. She curled up in the bed and pulled her blankets back around her shoulders. The sighing of the trees had quieted her. She began to drift off to sleep. She felt as if she were lying in a grove of big white pines. *How can that be?* She wondered, as she fell back into her dreams.

She awoke again just before dawn. The sound of pines swaying in the wind still filled her room. Interwoven with their quiet rustling came a voice calling her name. "Kelly. . . . Kelly. . . . Wake up." The voice spoke in the same whispering tone. "Do not be frightened, Kelly. I will not harm you."

Kelly's eyes searched the room, but she found no one there. Her heart pounded loudly, as if her chest might break with its hammering. She fought to control her fear so that it did not overwhelm her. She felt somewhat calmed by the wind in the trees, though she didn't know how the sound could be in her room.

"Kelly, please listen to what I have to say. There is no reason to be afraid," the voice said gently.

Sitting up in bed, Kelly asked, her voice trembling, "Who are you?"

"I apologize. I have not introduced myself. I am called Garth in your language. In my own tongue, you would not understand my name. I am the spokesperson for all of us. There are many of us, but not all can speak your language, though they understand your feelings and needs."

Kelly stood up and stared around the room. "There are many of you?"

"I speak for all of the ancient ones."

Kelly reached under her bed and pulled out her 28-inch Louisville Slugger and held it tightly in both hands. "Where are you? What are you talking about? The joke's over, and I don't think your little game is very funny." She swung the bat menacingly and kept talking, letting loose her pent-up fears. "You've been waking me up all week and scaring me half to death. I don't know who you are or where you are. I don't know how you got into this house, but you better get out, NOW!"

"We cannot leave this house. The house is made of us." The sighing of the wind in the boughs grew stronger. "I am sorry we frightened you. We are not here in jest. We come to you in desperation. We have been waiting for you for many years. We need your help. Please let me explain."

Kelly, still clutching her bat, started to tremble again. "What do you want?"

"I am Garth. I speak for the great white pines. I am here in this house as others of my kind are here; the house is made of white pine timber. We are fortunate to be here. So many others completely lost their lives in fires. We are the spirits of the ancient pines that once grew here. Your grandfather's grandfather built this house from us one hundred years ago. We have been waiting for you. We knew that you would come and would understand."

"I've lived here for five years, and you never spoke to me before," Kelly stammered.

"We have waited for you to come of age. Until now we could only draw you to this room, but you wouldn't have understood our need."

"If you are here, why can't I see you?"

"You look at us all the time. You just don't know what you are seeing. We are here."

Kelly looked around the room. She still held the bat. Her hands were cold with fright, and her stomach felt tight and knotted. "Where?"

"In the wood, dear child. In the heartwood of this room, of this house. Come here and stand before me. Come to the double doors."

Kelly slowly walked across her room.

"I am here, in this shape that you have called 'the monk.'"

"Oh, my gosh. You're alive in there!" Kelly's eyes were riveted on the hooded, dark figure in the wood paneling. "And the others," she said, pointing at the dark figures that encircled her walls. "Are they alive, too?"

"Those that you so thoughtfully named, yes, they are ancient ones. You knew somewhere deep within you that they were alive."

"I thought their eyes sometimes followed me. And when I was sad, they seemed sad, too." She turned back to the door. "But Monk, I mean Garth, you have seemed very sad for a long, long time."

"This burden of sadness is why we have awakened you to our calling. We need your help."

Kelly looked at him blankly. "What kind of help?"

"It is long and difficult to explain. It will take time for you to understand. But you are our only hope."

"What can I do to help you? I'm only twelve!"

Garth's voice took on new warmth. "You have much more knowledge than you think. You are strong and gifted. You have the sight, and you know the woodlands and pathways. The trails that lie in the land have been traced upon your memory. You will always know where the paths lead, even when the way cannot be seen."

She looked at him. "What do you mean?"

"Help will come to you in ways you cannot understand now, on pathways that are forgotten. But it is morning and you must start your day. Tonight we will speak again."

"Where will these pathways lead me?"

"You must go into the past."

"Garth! Garth? What do you mean?"

But the hooded monk was silent.

Chapter 2
The Sharing

Grandma set down her mug and looked across the table at her granddaughter. "Kel, are you feeling all right?"

Kelly looked up from her cereal and blinked. She brushed her hair back from her forehead. "Grandma, I'm fine."

Grandma shook her head and scrutinized Kelly's face. "You seem very distracted and tired this morning. Didn't you sleep well?"

Kelly sighed. "Oh, Grandma. I had some strange dreams again. Different from the other ones. But, I'm feeling okay. I just need to shake off those dreams."

Grandpa reached over and touched her cheek. "Your grandma's right. You do seem a bit quiet this morning."

Kelly stretched her arms and yawned. "I'm just thinking about what to pack for camping. I want to get going, and I thought maybe we could have Sara come with us. But she e-mailed and said she's going

to go with her mom to visit her aunt and uncle and won't be back for a week."

"It would have been fun to have Sara with us. But, camping? Not with all this rain. We are not going anywhere today." He sipped his tea. "We can certainly pack our gear and get ready for tomorrow." His eyes sparkled.

"Yeah!" Kelly exclaimed.

Grandma turned to her husband. "Evan, if Kelly's feeling at all under-the-weather you two should postpone your trip. I don't want you out in the middle of nowhere with a sick girl."

"Aw Grandma, I'm not sick. See. . . ." Kelly jumped up and danced a jig around the table. Grandpa and Grandma both laughed.

Grandma got up and hugged Kelly. "I guess you are fine, and you can get ready for that trip of yours." She kissed Kelly's forehead. "Right now I've got to leave for Eagle Creek or I'll be late."

After breakfast, Grandpa Evan and Kelly planned their camping trip. They agreed to wait until the weather cleared. As they were writing out a list of "things to do," Kelly turned to her grandfather. "Grandpa, I thought it cleared off last night, and the moon came out."

"It could only have been in your dreams, Kel. The rain fell all night long." He had rolled the tent out on the living room floor and was inspecting the seams. "You said you had strange dreams. Did you have any more nightmares?"

"No. No more nightmares. I just had some weird dreams about the wind in the trees and the moon shining in my room." She handed him the seam seal for the tent.

"Well, that sure is a lot better than those freezing cold dreams you've had the past few nights." He knelt on the rug and squeezed the tube along the tent edge. "I bet you were surprised to see it still raining though," he chuckled. "Maybe in your dreams you were camping under the stars." He straightened up. "We'll try to make that dream come true tomorrow."

Kelly gave him the thumbs up sign. *I hope so,* she thought. *I want to get away from my room and Garth.*

For most of the day they organized their gear. Sleeping bags and pads, stove, cooking gear, food, and first-aid kit all had to be checked out and packed. Grandpa Evan always insisted on carrying extra food, in case of an emergency. "Now, Kel, do you have your essential gear?" Grandpa's essential gear included waterproof matches, compass, pocketknife, and bug spray, in addition to clothing.

"Yes, it's all right here." She held up a small nylon bag. "Except for my clothes; I still have to pack them. But I can do that later."

"Pack for the predicted weather—cold weather clothes, hot weather clothes, warm weather clothes, rain gear!" he declared.

Kelly laughed. "I see you're taking the weatherman's word and trusting his prediction, as usual."

"Well, you can never be too sure." Evan slumped into an overstuffed chair. "This old man's getting worn out. What are we going to do if it rains tomorrow?"

"Fly to Jamaica," Kelly responded, her blue eyes laughing; Grandpa called them her Irish eyes. She threw a pillow at him. "Think of the hot sun and the big sand beaches. Sara told me they don't even have bugs there."

"It sounds like paradise, but who needs it? We'll take the mosquitoes any day. Right?" His thick eyebrows arched over his own vivid Irish eyes. He paused, waiting for a response, and finally gave it himself. "Right." He threw the pillow back at her.

"Oh, you know I was just kidding." She got up and walked toward the kitchen. "What about dinner? I'm hungry."

"A bit of dinner sounds good to these weary bones." He stood up and followed her into the kitchen. "Ann will be home soon, and she's going to be tired and hungry, too, especially after tramping about in the rain all day. Maybe I'll make some chili."

"Great. You know it's one of Grandma's favorites."

After dinner, Kelly decided to pack her clothes. She climbed the stairway slowly, reluctant to go into her room. "Hey Kel, get a move on it. You'll never finish packing at that rate," Evan called from below. She bounced up the last few steps and down the hall. But she slowed again as she approached her door. *You must go into the past,* the voice nagged at the back of her mind.

This is ridiculous, she thought. *I shouldn't be afraid to go into my own room.* Her hand rested on the doorknob. She turned it, gave a quick push, and stepped inside. The room seemed just the way it always had. Kelly glanced around, but avoided looking in Garth's direction. She opened her closet and began pulling out her gear for the trip. "Better oil these boots tonight," she murmured to herself.

"They look like they could use some oiling," said a voice behind her. She jumped.

"Sorry, Kel. I didn't mean to startle you, but Grandma thought you might need to pack this jacket. You left it in the hall closet." Grandpa Evan set the jacket on the bed. "Are you all right?"

"Sure. I'm just a little tired."

"It's early to bed for us tonight," he said as he walked to the door.

Kelly stood up. "Grandpa, I'm not *that tired.* Can the three of us play a game?"

"Come on downstairs when you're through and we'll see." He headed down the hall.

Kelly turned around. She could feel the eyes of Garth and the others staring at her. She remembered him saying, "Do not be frightened. I will not harm you." She sighed. Picking up her boots and her clothes, she walked out of her room. Garth's voice seemed to echo softly behind her, mixed with the sound of pines in a breeze, "Tonight we will speak again."

They played several rounds of UNO, with Grandma winning once, and Kelly taking the second and third sets. "Grandpa, are you sure you don't want another chance to beat us?" Kelly asked hopefully.

"Count me out," Grandma said as she pushed her chair away from the table. "I'm leaving early in the morning to meet with that botanist from Ashland. Off to bed with me."

"We had better follow Ann's wise example, Kel."

"I'd like to sleep down here on the couch," Kelly said as she stretched out on the cushions.

Grandpa laughed. "Sleep and that lumpy couch do not go together. It's off to bed and a good night's sleep for you."

If only they knew, Kelly thought.

She turned off the light and snuggled down in bed, hoping that the image of Garth and the others would simply fade away into the night. The darkness closed in around her, her body tense with fear. Slowly the sound of the pines began to fill the room. Though Kelly tried to remain alert, she began to relax to the rhythm of the wind.

As the wind surrounded her, she fell into the softness of its calling. Deeper and deeper she slipped toward sleep. At the edge of dreams she heard Garth's voice. "Go to sleep, child. Go to sleep and dream of the visions that we send you."

A grove of gigantic pines towered above the hillside. Their black trunks blended into the night; moonlight played on their branches. Kelly leaned against the rough bark of a tree. The earth smelled of spring, and the air held warmth instead of cold. But where was she?

The moon lit a pathway amongst the trees. Kelly got up and followed this silvery path. It seemed to lead right into the heart of the moon. The trees surrounding her rose tall and straight, bigger than any she had ever seen.

The path beckoned her on, winding among the trees and climbing a ridge. Kelly struggled up the steep hillside. At the top, the trail seemed to end in a pool of light. She stopped and looked around. The moon had risen higher and now shone almost directly down on her. She looked up and saw that she stood near the base of an enormous tree. She gasped at its height. She rested her hand in a deep seam in the corky trunk. Slowly she became aware of the sound of a breeze high up in the top of the tree. "Kelly." A voice tumbled down to her. "I wanted you to see me as I was. Yes, I am Garth, here in my home. We are surrounded by the others. We are a part of the mighty grove of pines that once stretched across much of the land of the Great Lakes. We were the jewels of the forest, lit by the moon and sun. We were strong then, and some of us grew to be five hundred years old. We were ancient and yet full of life. The wisdom of the ages grew in our hearts." The breeze strengthened. "And that wisdom has been locked there ever since."

"Garth, you are so beautiful." Kelly turned slowly. "The entire forest is beautiful."

"Yes. But you haven't truly seen how vast and unbroken we were. Our true beauty lay in the whole of the land, not just in one tree or one hillside. We were glorious, unpredictable, and wild. When one died then, it was natural. There was grace and beauty in that death. Our wisdom, our character was passed on to the younger ones." He paused. "All of that is lost in your time. I thought perhaps if you could see this, you might begin to understand."

"Garth, is this the hillside to the north of my house?" Kelly asked.

"It is the same location, but it is different. So much has died and been forgotten. Between this time and your own, there has been great loss."

"I walked there the other day. The hill is covered with aspen and paper birch and some maple, and here and there you can find a small pine. But they are very young. It seemed that I came right to this very spot, as if I had been led here."

"You are standing on an old trail. As I told you last night, you can find the old routes. These are the trails used by the Native Peoples and later by the Voyageurs and other travelers throughout time. You have the power to feel them and know where they lead."

Kelly sighed. "But why? What good will it do for me to walk these old paths?"

"You cannot follow them now. It will do no good, for we are just in your dreams. We must go back together; you will lead me into the past. I am not able to seek out the Old Age on my own. But you and your grandfather and I shall journey together."

"Grandpa? Does he know about this, too?" she asked in amazement.

"He knows, but he has forgotten. As I have awakened you, you must awaken him."

"But how?"

"Last week you brought a large pine cone into your room and set it on your bookcase. Where did you find such a beauty?"

"I'd canoed over to Lookout Island. I found that cone beneath the biggest pine tree there, the one we call the Sentinel. Grandma says the trees there are truly ancient. And that cone is the biggest one I've ever found."

"Take that magnificent pine cone and give it to your Grandfather. It will spark some old, forgotten stories that are buried in his mind, memories that will help you both understand."

The wind began to dance in the boughs. Kelly's mind was filled with their whisperings. *Sleep. Sleep,* they seemed to say.

The rain beat furiously against the windowpanes. Grandpa shook his head and turned away from the window.

"Yesterday the forecast said it would be cleared off by now." He filled his teacup with hot water and noisily sat down in his chair. "Just look at that." He shook his finger at the window. "What is this, a monsoon?"

"Grandpa, take it easy. The weather'll clear soon enough. You always say the forecasts are wrong anyway, so it'll probably be beautiful by this afternoon." Kelly poured herself a bowl of cereal, adding milk and honey. "Do you want some cereal?"

Evan stopped fiddling with his tea bag and pulled it out of the cup. "Yes, I do, thanks." She handed him a bowl and spoon. "I'm sorry I'm such a grump," he said. "I know you've been looking forward to this trip for a long time. And I have, too."

"We'll have a great day anyway," Kelly said. "What time did Grandma leave for her meeting?"

"She was ready and gone by six o'clock. You know how excited she is about those plants they've found. And when she's interested in some fern or flower or anything that's green, well, she's raring to go. You know, it's especially important that these plants be identified and cataloged. This may help resolve the conflicts surrounding the mine and how it will operate."

Kelly nodded. "Grandma's really a terrific botanist. I love to see her so excited about her work." Kelly set a plate of toast on the table.

As Evan reached for the plate, he saw the pine cone sitting on the edge of the counter. "Kel, where did that come from? I don't know if I've ever seen one that large before."

"I got it on Lookout Island." She handed him the cone. "My friend Garth thought you might be interested in it."

"Garth? Can't say as you've ever mentioned him before." Evan turned the cone over in his hands and held it up to his nose. A strange look came over his face. "That pitchy aroma smells really rich and old." Evan looked puzzled. "Kel, who thought I might be interested in it?"

She answered, her voice steadier than she felt. "Garth." She looked at her grandfather. "He said that you would remember, and your recollections would help us understand."

Evan held the cone to his face again and breathed in the resinous memories. He sat silently for several minutes, deep in thought. Then he reached across the table and took her hand. "I think you'd better tell me everything that's been happening to you these past few days. I had no idea that Garth was awake again."

She told him about the dreams and the talks with Garth in the night. She described the previous evening's walk through the forest in the moonlight. The conversations she had with Garth came back to her mind clearly, and she repeated them easily. No detail of those encounters escaped her, and she was amazed at the power of her own memory. "That's everything, Grandpa," she said at last. "I thought I was just dreaming, but it felt so real."

His eyes searched hers. "You weren't dreaming at all. Garth is real, and I'm sure the need he speaks of is real, too. I should have known that he would try to speak with you. I should never have let you stay in that room, but I thought—no, I hoped—that he was just a legend, an old story made up by my father to amuse me as a child. And so I forgot about the stories and let them slip from my memory." He folded his hands. "I shouldn't have, though; I promised I wouldn't forget." There was a note of sadness in his voice.

"But have you forgotten them, Grandpa? Don't you still remember them?"

"I remember them now, but it's too late to stop them from haunting you. You shouldn't have been drawn into this. You're too young." He sighed. "But it was predicted, and how can I protect you from that?"

Now Kelly looked puzzled, "What do you mean, 'predicted'?"

"In the old stories, they always said the one who would come to help them would be the first grandchild born to the first son of the firstborn child in this house. No one thought much about it. In fact, hardly anyone knew about the prediction. And when I heard the story as a boy, I didn't have much concern for a possible grandchild. I was only a child then myself. But the child they spoke of is you. My father, Charles, your great-grandfather, was the firstborn child in this house. He was born the summer they finished the building. His room is now yours." Evan stopped and folded his arms over his chest.

"You see, Kel, because he was born here, the trees thought they could make him understand them. And he did understand them, but he couldn't really help them. It was an impossible time. There needed to be many years of change before the right person was to be born. The trees themselves predicted that my firstborn grandchild—and they said granddaughter—would be the one who would help them. They said one hundred years would lapse from the time the house was built of their logs to the year when you would arrive."

He held the cone in his hand, slowly turning it. "My father told me all of these tales, and I thought that's all they were. As I grew older, I forgot about them. But the night that you were born they came back to me, and I thought they were wrong, for when you were born, the house was 88 years old, not 100. I didn't think they meant to wait until you were older, to wait until the 100 years had passed, and you had come of age." He looked older as he sat there, as if the weight of the decades were pushing down on him.

"Grandpa, how can we go into the past as Garth has asked?" Kelly watched him rolling the cone over and over. "I still don't understand what he wants of us."

"I'm not too sure either, Kel, but we'll find out." He handed her the pine cone. "The answers lie in your room. Let's go see what we can find out."

They stood before the old oak desk in Kelly's room. Somehow it seemed larger than ever to Kelly and more mysterious. She had always felt that it belonged somehow to the realm of fairies and gnomes — or maybe to Sherlock Holmes, because of its hidden compartments and sliding panels.

Kelly watched her grandfather run his hands over the top. "Somewhere here is the lever that opens a compartment along the right side of the desk," he said, as his fingers slipped into the groove that ran down the front panel. "Let's see now. Where could it be?"

"I've found other hidden drawers in this desk, but not like the one you're looking for," Kelly said. "The others have always been very small, not large enough for a book." She followed his searching fingertips with her eyes.

He gently traced the initials, "C.O.," with his finger, "Yes. That's it!"

"Where?" Kelly leaned over him. "I don't see anything."

"Not yet. But watch. See how the "O" is etched into the wood? It's carved around a knot. Just like an eye, it seems to watch for the right person to come along and open up the drawer. It won't work for everyone, though. You must have the right touch."

Kelly stepped closer. "I never realized that knot was there, and I've looked at those carved letters closely. Are you the only one it will open for?"

"Well, up until now I am. But I suspect that after this, you'll be able to open it, too." He pressed his index finger over the center of the "O," and a panel slid open along the side of the desk.

"Look at that! You'd never know that could open." Kelly stood back while Evan peered inside the dark space. He reached in and withdrew two small booklets.

"These are my father's diaries. He wrote them when he was not much older than you are now." Evan reached into the cubicle again and pulled out a third volume. "This one he wrote later, a year or two before he died." He set the books down on the desktop. "I've never really read them, though I've known they were here for years." He dusted off one of the covers with the back of his hand. "You and I are the only ones who know these even exist."

"You never even told Grandma?" Kelly was shocked.

Evan sadly shook his head. "I didn't want it to be real. It frightened me when I was a child. Then I forgot about the stories as I grew older or pushed them out of my thoughts."

Kelly lined the three books on the edge of the desk. The books were bound in dark brown leather. She opened one, and her great-grandfather's black writing flowed across the lined pages like a winding current.

"Grandpa, didn't these notebooks make you curious? Didn't you ever want to read them?"

Evan pulled the chair out and sat down at the desk. "I was curious, but I guess I was frightened, too." He fingered the edge of one of the books. "I wasn't sure what was in these, and I kept wanting to believe that those old tales my dad told me were really nothing more than that. I was afraid that if I read the diaries, I'd find out more than I wanted to know." He paused. "I didn't want the past to haunt me."

Kelly set the diary down. "Maybe we should put them away and forget that they exist."

He reached out and took her hand. "No. We need to do this. Charles promised that this family would do all it could to help. My father pledged his son and great-grandchild would help, and so we must. The O'Malleys never go back on their word." He smiled at her. "Don't worry, Kel. I'm sorry I've been so serious about this. It's such a change. It just takes some getting used to." He laughed. "In fact, I think it's going to be quite an adventure."

Chapter 3
The Diaries

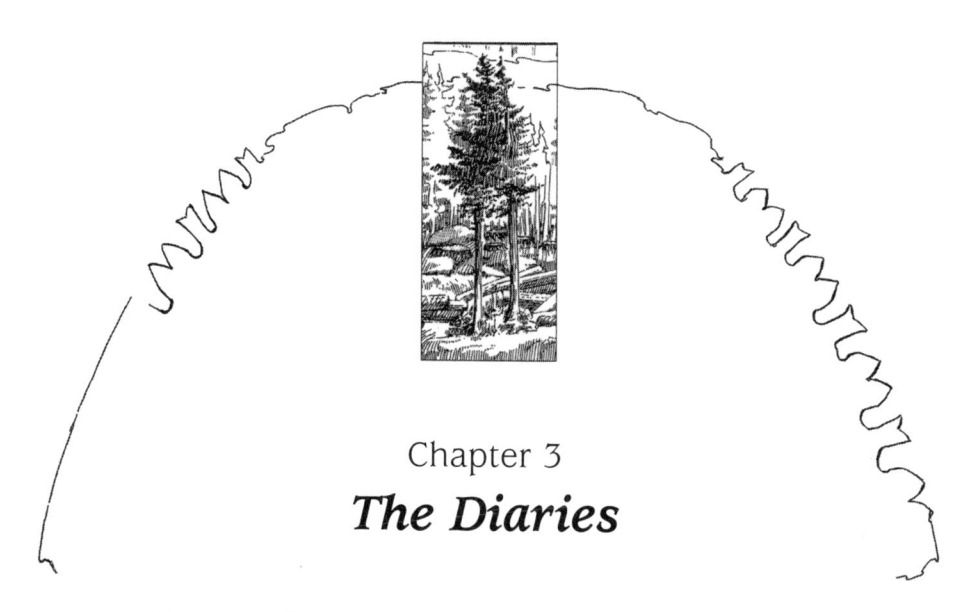

"Listen to this entry," Kelly said. "It's dated September 25, 1915." She paused. "That would make him twelve years old, like I am now." She was sitting cross-legged in front of the fireplace in the living room. Evan sat on the couch behind her with another diary in his hand. The daylight was rapidly draining out of the room as the grayness of twilight seeped in. Rain continued to splatter the windows, but its pattering was drowned out by the crackling of the fire.

"You know what else?" She continued without waiting for a response. "He sat right here in front of the fire and wrote this account. Can you believe that? That's just wild!"

"Well, he lived here, too, just like you do now. Only it was a long time ago." Her grandfather smiled at her. "What is so intriguing about September 25, 1915?"

"Just listen." She began to read the words of her great-grandfather.

"Today I explored the northern edge of the old Pinkerton 40. The trees were leveled, just as they are over most of this area. I could see from the river all the way over to Star Lake. Huge pine stumps littered the ground. The forest was decapitated. I

could see where massive slash piles had been burned. No big trees were left anywhere. All have been floated down stream. There was supposed to be an old trail through here that led to the pine ridge, but I couldn't find a trace of it.

"Perhaps what Garth said about the cuttings is true. It must have been frightening to see trees dying in all directions. And I am going to be a woodsman someday, too. How am I ever going to be able to cut those trees without seeing Garth standing before me?"

Kelly jumped up. "Grandpa! Put out the fire! We can't burn these logs."

"No, Kelly. We can burn wood. We live here, too. We need to use some of the resources that are here. All life forms give and take. We need to be sure we don't just take, but we also give back."

"But, Grandpa, we're murdering the trees."

"You could look at it that way, or you could look at the bigger picture. We aren't clear-cutting huge acreage as Charles was talking about. We selectively cut our forest. We replant. If we didn't burn wood, we'd have to burn something else—coal, fuel oil, natural gas."

"I guess so," she muttered.

"Kelly, everybody makes an impact. It's a matter of keeping your imprint on the planet as light as possible. Giving back. Trying to make the world better."

"Like helping Garth?"

"Maybe."

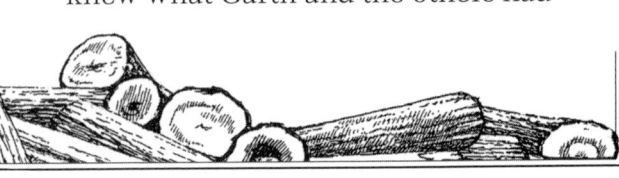

She sat down on the edge of the couch, still holding the open diary. "But, I can't believe this! This is so rotten! It makes me really mad!" She slapped the diary closed. "Great-grandpa knew what Garth and the others had gone through, but he couldn't help them. Worse yet, he knew he'd soon be out there cutting, too."

"I know it was difficult for him," Evan replied, "but he had to make a living. By the time he was a youngster, most of the big pines had been cut, and they were cutting the hardwoods and hemlocks. What was he going to do—go to his father and tell him that he'd been talking with the trees and they wanted the cutting stopped? His father, from all I have been able to understand, would never have stood for any wild stories such as that. He'd have been thrashed to within an inch of his life." Evan opened the diary in his hand. "This is what my father wrote years later about his boyhood."

"Life here in this house ran from one extreme to another. Dad was always working, and we were always out working with him, especially me, being the oldest. I learned the ways of the woodsman early. From a youngster on, I was out with the cutters and work teams. Some winters I worked in the stable with the horses or worked as a cookie in the cook shack. Sometimes, in the winters, I hauled water for the ice roads.

"But when we were here at home, I was always torn between my father and his work and the tales that I was learning from Garth. I wanted to help them both, but how could I? When Garth sent me into the past, I just wanted to stay there and never come back."

Kelly looked amazed. "You mean that Great-grandpa traveled into the past also?"

Evan laughed. "Yes he did. Judging by the tales he told me when I was young, he went several times." He pointed at the diaries. "Maybe these will tell about some of those trips. We'll need to find those entries. Maybe they'll help us."

They both settled back with their reading. Kelly jumped up when the phone rang. "I'll get it, Grandpa." She ran to the kitchen. "Yes, Grandma," she was saying as she returned to the living room. "Do you want to talk with him?" She paused and frowned, "No, we'll be fine. I hope you get all of the paperwork finished." She listened a few moments. "Okay. Bye."

Grandpa Evan set down his journal. "Well?"

"She and Jan are trying to get some plants identified and processed with the lab in Madison. They need to have all of the forms faxed in by noon tomorrow." Kelly crossed the room and sat down on the sofa.

"How late did she think she'd be?"

"I don't know, but she said not to wait up." Kelly picked up the diary she'd been reading.

Grandpa Evan smiled. "You know how carried away she and Jan can get over plants, and this mine issue is really fueling their fire. I guess you'll just have to put up with me all evening."

The evening wore on into darkness. Evan stacked more wood on the fire and heated a pot of water on the stove. He came back from the kitchen with two mugs of cocoa. "Here Kelly," he said, handing her a cup and sinking into the easy chair with the other.

Kelly stirred her cocoa. "If Charles traveled into the past, why couldn't he have helped Garth then? What do the trees need us for?"

"I'm not sure, but I think he was too close to the situation. He was caught in the middle. He felt he could either help the trees or help his family, but he couldn't do both. He thought that if he helped Garth, he would be placing his family in jeopardy." He set his cup down. "Listen to this last entry."

"Garth told me that if I didn't help them, no one could – not until decades had passed and my oldest son had a granddaughter. I was twelve years old and was told that my great-granddaughter was the only hope they would have. What was I supposed to do? I finally told Garth that I wouldn't return to the past again. So I have left this burden with a child of the future. I hope she will be stronger than I was.

"As I have grown older, I have begun to see that Garth was right. The forests have changed in a way that no one can ever understand who didn't see them in their original wildness. They were our greatest living sanctuary, equal parts museum, church, and encyclopedia all wrapped up in a place so beautiful you held your breath. I don't even recognize the landscape anymore. There is despondency in the forests, a sense of loss so profound. . . why it's like we burned our history books. Most of those ancient pines that once graced this land are forever gone, along with the wisdom of their race and age. Nearly all of the trees of today have no deep historical roots, no understanding of their heritage. In a way, they have lost their heartwood.

"We, too, have lost our heart. We lost it when we laid this land bare and didn't give it a second thought. I pray that Evan's grandchild will bring the heart back to this land."

Evan closed the book and looked into the flames.

Kelly stared into them, too. Her journey into the past would be in the footsteps of this great-grandfather that she had never known. She wondered if she could do any better than he had done.

Kelly slept deeply that night without dreaming of the woodlands and Garth. She woke well-rested and hungry. It was then that she realized they'd been so involved in the diaries that they hadn't eaten any dinner. She hopped out of bed, dressed, and headed down to the kitchen where she was greeted by the smell of frying pancakes and hot blueberries.

She eyed the table with delight. "What a way to start the day!"

Evan hugged her. "Good morning, Kel. Sleep well last night?"

"You bet, Grandpa. I can't remember a single dream."

"Sit yourself down and eat. I thought I might have to turn the radio on full blast to wake you up." He handed her a plate of pancakes. "Will you get the hot syrup from the microwave?"

Kelly set the pitcher on the table. "Where's Grandma?"

"Oh, she's on the Internet already." He walked to the doorway. "Ann, breakfast is ready, and Kelly is threatening to eat all of your pancakes if you don't come soon!"

Grandma Ann entered the kitchen and kissed the top of Kelly's head. "How is our youngest camper this morning?"

Kelly smiled. "I'm great—look at how beautiful it is this morning." She poured more syrup on her cakes. "How are you, Grandma? Did you finish your work so you can go camping with us?"

"I'm sorry, but this research is very pressing right now. It's so important to get these plants cataloged." She held up a slip of paper. "I came across this John Muir quote this morning that just made me want to work harder. Do you want to hear it?"

"Sure," Kelly replied.

"'They tell us plants are perishable, soulless creatures, that only man is immortal, but this, I think, is something that we know very nearly nothing about.'" She looked across the table at Kelly. "I need to finish this work. I can't join you this time, but when you get back in a few days I should be finished."

Kelly set down her fork and swallowed. "Grandma, if you need to get this done, it's okay. I mean, I'd rather have you with us, but I know how important this project is." She grinned a purple-blueberry smile. "Besides, I can keep an eye on Grandpa."

"Hey," Grandpa Evan said gruffly, "I don't need anyone to keep an eye on me!"

"You're right," Ann agreed. "Kelly, you'd better keep two eyes on your grandfather!"

After Ann left, Evan and Kelly were cleaning up the kitchen when Evan said, "Garth may not have found his way into your dreams, but he sure has found a way into mine. From the dreams that I had, I think we need to discuss some things with Garth soon."

Later, when they entered Kelly's room, they were greeted by the sound of the wind in the pines. "I am glad that you have come to talk," Garth said. "I have waited a long time for this honor, Evan. Your father was a fine man. I knew his son would be of the same wisdom."

"But Great-grandpa didn't help you," Kelly said.

"He did in his own way. He gave as much as he could. He gave us hope for the future."

Evan pulled out the chair by the desk, and Kelly sat down on the bed. "Garth, how do we begin?" Evan asked. "My father pledged our support, but I have no idea how we can help you."

Garth's voice came softly through the wind. "Together we will travel. I will show you the beauty and the spirit of the land. Thus our work shall begin. Bring your gear and let us be off. We have much to do."

"But how can we go with you?" Kelly asked.

"Are you not packed and ready for travel? Yes, I know you are. Just bring your equipment, and we shall leave."

WESTERLY BREEZES　　　　TAKE ME HOME

Chapter 4
The Four

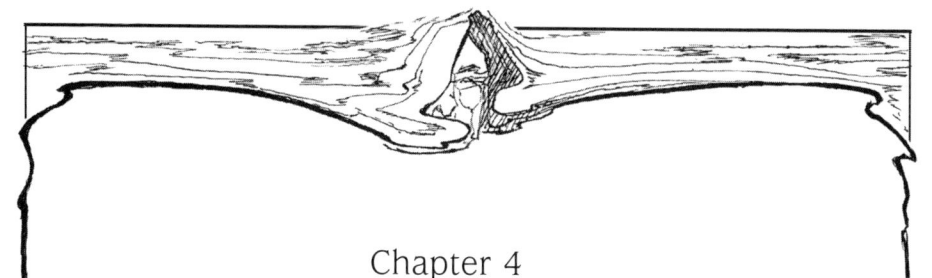

Evan and Kelly returned shortly to the bedroom with their gear. They had changed into their hiking clothes and held their packs. Kelly looked at her grandfather nervously.

Garth spoke gently. "There is no reason to be afraid. Charles felt nervous on his first trip, but he soon got over that. Now come close. Each of you must place a hand on the wood of my robe."

They walked to the doors and did as Garth asked them. "Now repeat this: 'Westerly breezes take us home.'" As the three spoke, Garth's dark robe danced out from the wood and encircled them all. Kelly felt a cold breeze on her face. Then she stood alone in a globe of darkness pierced by thousands of stars. The stars formed constellations she couldn't remember, though they seemed familiar. The sky lightened, the stars faded, and warmth returned.

A hermit thrush sang in the distance. Kelly and Evan found themselves on a path in a deep forest. Standing with them was a tall, shadowy, dark-cloaked figure. As he turned to face them, Kelly saw deep brown eyes set in sharp features. He looked like a man with his dark, hawk-like face and his black flowing hair. He seemed to be young and old all at once, with a slight smile upon his lips. The deep brown pools of his eyes shone like ancient, deeply set stones of tiger's-eye. "We have arrived," Garth said.

Kelly gasped when she looked at her Grandpa. "What's happened to us?"

Garth said, "You are fine. There is nothing wrong with you or with your gear. But when one passes through the Portals of Time, one's belongings and clothing become of that time period." He gestured to her clothing. "You are dressed as a traveler in this century, and your belongings are of this era, also."

Evan laughed. "I guess we couldn't very well travel about in our fleece jackets and convertible pants without attracting attention. People might wonder about our hiking boots and Gore-Tex rain gear." He looked at Kelly. "You look absolutely lovely in your calico dress and moccasins."

"Well, we won't be calling Grandma on our cell phone will we?" Kelly laughed.

"No. I don't think it's going to be that kind of trip, Kel."

"Your grandmother will be fine," Garth said. "You will be surprised to find how little time actually passes in your era while you journey into another time." Garth picked up one of their packs. "You will find that everything you need is still in your packs, only it has been changed to reflect this time."

The trail ran off in a northwesterly direction, winding through the pines. The trees spread their branches in graceful layers as the dark trunks rose skyward. Near their tops, the sun shone down through the branches, creating a tapestry of greens and light. Kelly felt very small standing amongst these giants. "Do they all have spirits?" she asked, motioning toward the trees.

Garth placed a strong, gnarled hand on her shoulder. "Of course they do. All living things have spirits. You couldn't live without a spirit to guide you. You will meet these tree spirits later. But let us be off." He turned and strode down the path. Evan and Kelly followed closely behind.

The trail dipped and curved, and they hiked along its reaches, soaking in the deep, muted colors of the forest. A rich, piney smell filled the air, and they breathed its fragrance and felt invigorated. The land rolled and the ridges came more frequently. The hikers began to climb. The hillsides grew steeper, with deeply cut valleys. Vegetation grew thickly in the sheltered glens. Kelly wished she could slow down and explore them. Garth kept a constant pace, and they steadily moved northward.

After a strenuous uphill climb, Garth bade them to follow him off the trail. They climbed a rock outcropping that covered the crest of the hill, and when they reached its peak, they stopped in amazement. From their vista, the land rippled on to the north. In the distance, they could see sunlight glimmering on a great expanse of water. "The great jewel of the north," Garth explained. "Many titles have been bestowed upon it in many tongues: Ke-che-gum-me, Lac de Trace, Cha-jik-o-ming, Father of Lakes, and in your own time, Lake Superior."

"It is more beautiful here in this time than I could have imagined," Evan said softly, gazing into the distance.

"Many changes have come to this region over the centuries. But since her forming, the lake has dominated all in her beauty, and in her anger as well," Garth replied. "She has drawn many to her, and some she has kept for her own." He turned in the opposite direction and pointed back the way they had come. "The view to the south beckons also."

The beauty of the woodlands gently rolled southward away from them, like an ocean of green waves. In the distance they could see marshes and small lakes carved into the woods. "This ridge runs closely parallel to the lake, but never gets too close to her. It is as if the ridge were shadowing the lake's movements. All along the crest, there are rock balds where plants have failed so far to establish themselves. The balds provide wonderful views of the land and lake. They still do in your time," Garth said, "though some time after this, the area was mined."

"Is this part of our Penokee Range?" Evan asked.

"Yes. This comes to be known as that. I believe it was in the 1850s that one of your geologists named the range after the Native name for iron, *penokie*. Iron is a great force in this rock." Garth gestured to a rock outcrop. "Perhaps that would be a pleasant spot to enjoy your lunch."

"My feet hurt," Kelly said as she sank down on the rock outcropping.

"I think it will take a few days to adjust to moccasins," Grandpa replied as he struggled out of his pack.

They relaxed on the overlook and ate their meal of pemmican, a mixture of dried meat and berries pounded together. "I think it'll take a few days to adjust to this, too," laughed Kelly.

At the edge of the clearing Garth sat straight-backed in quiet contemplation.

When lunch was over, Garth turned to them. "We will hike no further today, for there is much we need to discuss. I have chosen to bring you here, for this vista will give you a good sense of the lay of the land. Here, it all spreads out at your feet." He stood up, and his arm swept in a circle about them. "You will need to know where the lakes and rivers flow and where the swamps and thickets may block your passage. You will need to know the route back to the grove of trees where we entered. That is the grove where I am at home and where the Council of the Ancient Ones convenes."

Garth gathered his cloak about him and sat once again on the rock facing Kelly and Evan. "There are several things you will need to remember on your journey."

"But," Kelly said, "aren't you going to be with us?"

He shook his head. "I can only be with you part of the time. You will be on your own."

"Why?" Kelly asked. "I thought you said we'd be traveling together?"

"I would like to accompany you, but I am bound to my wood in the past. I cannot leave for long periods of time. In fact, I must return before evening." He smiled at them. "But I can come to you much easier than you imagine. There are other portals I can travel through without having to walk as you do. I can travel from site to site within moments. Thus, I will be with you as often as you need me. If you need me at any time on this journey, send my name out along the rivers or along the trails, and I shall hear of your calling and come to you."

They watched him intently as he continued. "There are several things for you to remember. First, the Portals of Time. You may travel between any time periods, from your own to any others in the past and between those of the past also. To travel between times, you must find the portals and pass through them. I cannot explain to you where these portals are, but you will know where to find them when you need them.

"Remember also that when you travel into another era, you are within that time. Do not linger there; for the longer you remain in the past, the greater the danger that you will become part of that time forever. You are still of your own time, but that time is now in the future. Do not get caught in the times of the past. You must pass through them to accomplish the quest." Garth repeated, "If you linger there too long, the portal will shut, and there you will remain."

Kelly felt a shiver rise up her back, and Evan put an arm around her shoulder. "Are you all right?" She nodded.

"When the Council meets," Garth continued, "it meets In-Between Time. It is not within your present or the past. If you ever need to step out of time, take these and use them." He handed Evan a packet of small seeds. "These will send you into the In-Between Time, and there the Council may help you."

Evan turned the tiny package over in his hand. Garth touched him on the shoulder. "They are precious. Only use them when all else has failed." Evan tucked the packet safely away in an inner pocket. "Evan, your knowledge of history and the woodlands will be very important on this journey." He took Kelly's hand within his. "And Kelly, the knowledge you possess of the routes, the portals, and the woods will help you many times. Though you may not know all of these things in your conscious mind, let that knowledge come through you. Do as your spirit directs."

Evan looked at Garth. "We've read the journals, and I remember my father's stories. But, I still don't know what we're searching for."

"You seek the Four of the Past for the Council. For this seeking to begin, you must go north. The Four will bring strength and unity. The Council, with the Four of the

Past, shall enable the trees in your time to grow in understanding and peace once again. Trees of your time have little knowledge of the past. But with the Four, the wisdom and spirit of the past may help the seeds of those future trees. It is as your father wrote, Evan. Most of the forests of your time do not mature. They grow little heartwood. While the ancient pines are forever gone, we hope to begin our restoration with this quest." Garth rose. "I must be off. Camp down in one of the dells south of the ridge tonight. Tomorrow you will start to the north."

Evan stood up. "Who or what are the Four that we seek?"

"Tonight you will meet the Council. Study the lay of the land." With a whirl of his cloak, Garth vanished.

Darkness had absorbed the remaining flickers of sunlight, and the stars had begun to come out. Kelly and Evan were talking beside the campfire when they heard the swoosh of Garth's cloak. "It is time," he announced. They stood and Garth wrapped the cloak around them, and they were gone into the coldness and stars.

A humming sound filled Kelly's ears, and when the cloak withdrew from her shoulders, she could see the Council of the Ancient Ones. Trees and other spirits like Garth were gathered in a circle in the grove. She could not tell the difference between some of them; the trees and their spirits seemed to blend together, as if they were one entity. The humming sounds came from the trees. *They must be talking,* she realized.

"We have arrived," Garth stated, and the humming ceased. He turned and introduced his companions. "This is the honorable Evan O'Malley and his granddaughter, Kelly. Evan is the son of Charles, and he brings with him the grandchild whose help was predicted a century past."

Garth bowed to them and then to the Council. "May I present to our guests the Council of Ancient Ones." Evan and Kelly bowed in return, and Kelly thought she could see some of the trees nodding to her. Looking down, Kelly realized she had her own clothing on once again, and so did her grandfather.

"They have seen the ridge and overlooks," Garth was saying, "and they are willing to start north tomorrow. But their quest must be defined for them."

The grove was softly illuminated. Beyond the trees it grew shadowy and dark as if the night were held back from this gathering. Kelly noticed many different trees: She saw white pines, hemlocks, spruces, sugar maples, as well as yellow birches with their curling golden bark. Within the circle of trees there was warmth, and she felt secure and safe. The sound of pine branches swaying in a breeze drifted down from somewhere high above. In the distance, a pair of wolves howled as if carrying on an eerie conversation.

A tall figure emerged from the grove, and his low voice broke through the quiet. "Greetings. I am called Westron. I have been asked by the others to tell you of the quest and ask your help."

Garth bade Evan and Kelly to come forward and sit on the ground near the center of the grove. He spread his cloak upon the ground and sat with them. Westron said, "We ask you to seek the Four of the Past and return with them to this Council." His voice strengthened as he began to chant, "The Four of the Past, the Four of the Past." Soon he was singing. Kelly felt as if she were in a cathedral. As Westron's song blended more and more with the wind, Kelly lay down and quickly fell asleep. In her dreams, images of the Four came alive, and she saw where they needed to travel to seek them.

She saw water—a pure and crystal-clear river with light dancing in it. The water ran from a huge, fresh ocean of water. The sun shone brightly upon it, and she could see ice fields to the north with rivers flowing out of them.

The dream changed and moved. The sun spiraled through the sky, and a ball of sunlight burst out from it and seared into the earth. The earth smoldered and burned, but rains came and quenched the fire. In the pit where the sunlight and earth had collided, a hard, coppery pool had formed that shone like the sun, but was as hard as rock.

Again the dream changed and whirled. All she could see was the sky stretching from horizon to horizon. The air smelled fresh and crisp like a frosty autumn morning. Clouds drifted through, and she found dragons and faces and animals in their shapes. The sky cleared. Day turned to night, and still she could smell the crispness of the air. It filled her body with life. Out of the night sky a single white feather drifted down to her, and in the moonlight a bird flew off into the darkness. Kelly bent and picked up the feather; it was cold and silvery-white.

The dreams whirled again and Kelly found herself along the edge of a forest. Birds sang airy, delicate tunes. A breeze rolled through the upper branches of the trees. Spring peepers rifled the air with their calls, and a squirrel rattled on a branch. Far away a wolf howled. She listened for a long while.

When Kelly awoke, the sun was beginning to peek down into the valley. Its first rays lit the dew on her fur sleeping robe, turning it into thousands of tiny jewels. "Grandpa," she whispered to the dark form across from her. "Wake up! Today we head north!"

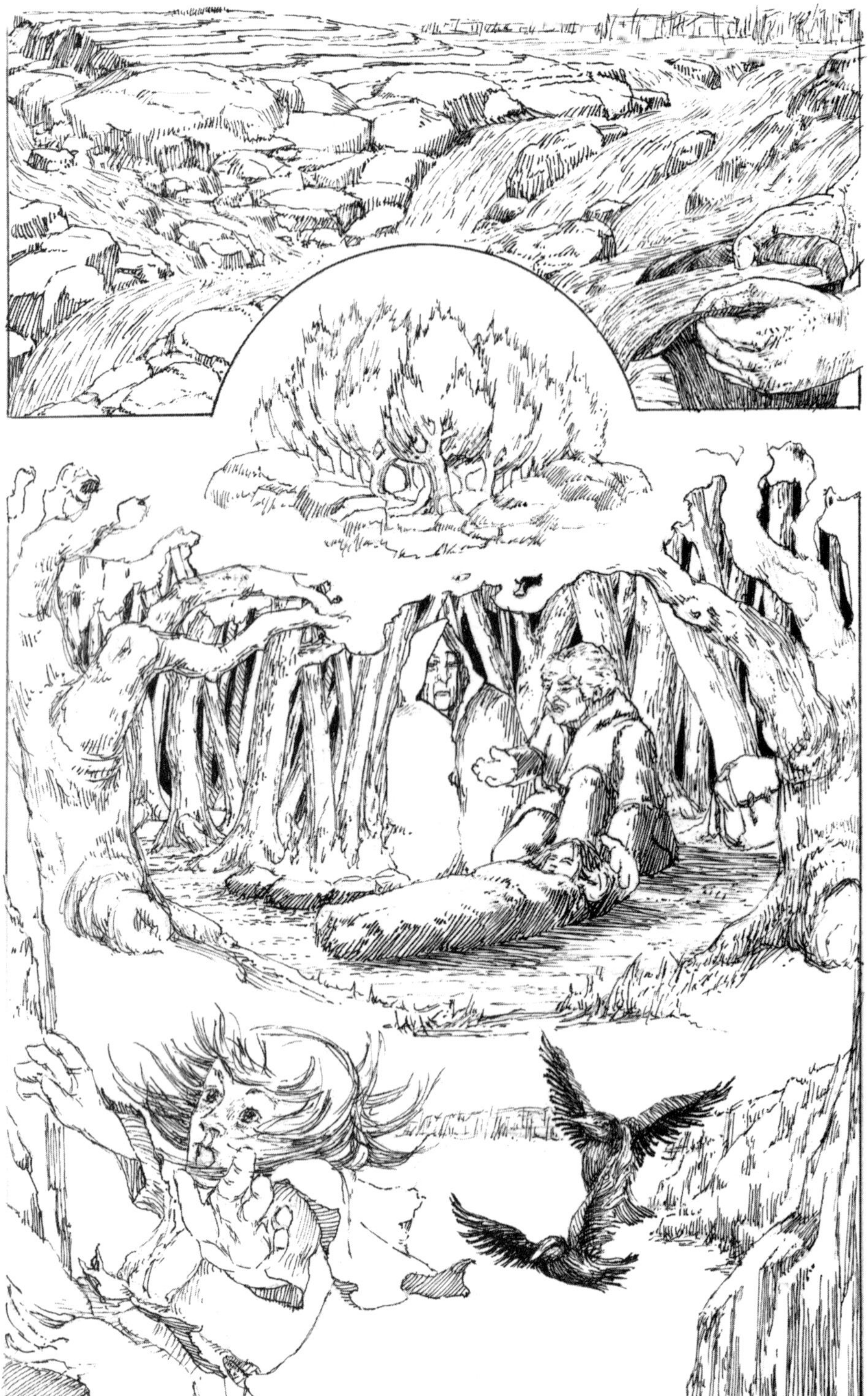

Chapter 5
Purity - The Beginning

Evan stopped and checked the ground. "I can't seem to find any trace of that trail through here. Have you found anything over there?" He received no response and called again. "Kel, have you found the trail?"

"Not really," Kelly called back. "But I think this is the right way, through the cedar swamp over there." She motioned toward the right. "I'm not sure how we lost the trail. I really think it just dissolved into the earth with no trace. I can't see it, but I can feel it in those woods."

Evan struggled through the undergrowth and joined her. "It does seem to have just disappeared. But you have a feeling about the cedar stand?"

Kelly nodded and started walking, pushing the tangled branches of the alders out of her way as she went. The small supple branches snapped at her face and grabbed at her clothing. They swung back behind her as she pushed through, working her way toward the stand of trees, Evan following behind.

She looked at Evan. "Why would anyone have ever put a trail through an alder swamp?"

Evan thought for a moment. "It may have been higher ground then. I suspect a beaver dam has flooded the area since, and now it's half under water."

Finally they both stood free of the brush, under the protective branches of a huge white cedar tree. The cedar swamp spread out before them, the shredding trunks of the cedar spiraling skyward. The forest was cooler and quieter, as if insulated from the outside world by its layers of cushioning branches. No birds sang here, and no chiding voices of squirrels rained down upon them. The ground was an interwoven net of moss-covered roots and small cavities of water. Here and there, a path seemed to emerge as an avenue through the trees.

"All of these could be paths," Evan said as he pointed to several of the more pronounced openings in the wood. "But, which one is right?"

Kelly had started ahead of him down one of the routes, then turned and came back. She sat down on a boulder near him. "That wasn't right. Maybe we're lost." She rested her chin on her hand and closed her eyes. *Relax. Relax,* she told herself. She let her mind drift and felt the past slowly seep into her consciousness. Yes, this is the way that would have been used—not over the far ridge, but right through here. But to where? Her mind would give her no answer except to follow the route she knew was there.

She opened her eyes. Evan was beside her. "Kel, are you feeling all right?"

"I have a headache. But I think I know the way, at least for a little while. We need to head through there." She pointed to the right. "Toward that next boulder." She slid off the rock. "Ready to head out?" He nodded at her and she walked ahead. She stopped. She turned toward Evan and smiled. "Yes, this is the way. It feels right."

Since leaving Garth, they had been hiking for three days, generally in a northerly direction. But they had run into numerous springs and bogs they hadn't seen from the ridge top, and so their progress was slow. Once deep into the cedar glade, the route opened up and they were able to walk easily amongst the large trees. The branches blocked out the sunlight, so small shrubs and saplings found it difficult to grow.

Kelly led them through the cedars, but the glade appeared to go on for miles. After they had been walking for an hour or more, she abruptly stopped. "Grandpa, the trail seems to veer off sharply to the left. Do you think that could be right?"

"All we can do in here, Kel, is to follow your feelings. If you think it turns left, that's the way we had better go." He looked ahead of her. "Well, I can see why you'd rather keep going north." The new route led away from the cedars and into a dense undergrowth of alders. "We'd best push on. We have a long way to go to get to the lake," Evan said.

She shrugged and headed west. "Kel," Evan said, "Why don't you let me go ahead for a while? You can always tell me if we're going off course, and I think I can find us a trail through that brush."

"Thanks. You know how I hate to bushwhack through that stuff." She stepped aside and let him take the lead. "I'm getting tired. These moccasins are okay, but they don't give my feet much support."

Evan called back to her. "You're just a tenderfoot, and you're not in condition yet!" He laughed.

"Oh Grandpa, I bet your feet are just as sore."

"Never!" he said as he entered the alders. The shrubs rose before them like a dense, woven mat of green and brown. "Onward through the fog!" He laughed again.

After battling their way through the brush for what seemed like forever to Kelly, Evan stopped. "I think I know where this leads. Are we still keeping close to the route?"

"Ever since we entered the cedar grove, the feeling about the route has been different. It's not as strong as it was in the pines, but I think it's still the right way for us to go." She stretched her arms. "I want to get out of here."

"I think we're just about to do that." He pointed to the ground. "See how wet it's getting?"

"Sure. My feet are getting soaked. Yuck." Mud was oozing around her moccasins. The leather was drenched through. "Grandpa, let's go."

"I promise it won't be long now." He paused. "I think I hear rushing water." As they hiked on, the ground became more and more spongy. Brush surrounded them like a prickling blanket, entangling their arms and legs.

Suddenly they emerged from the brush. "Oh, my!" Kelly gasped. They stood at the edge of a wild river. The current curled the surface of the water as it raced by them, around the boulders and on down the river.

Evan surveyed the riverbank. "This must be our route north to the lake. What do you think?"

Kelly did not answer. As she watched the water racing past her, the dream of a clear river with sunlight dancing in it came swiftly into her mind. Cold, pure water washed through her thoughts. "This is the way, Grandpa, but it's the wrong time." Her face paled and she shivered. "The portal lies downstream, around the bend."

Evan thought for a moment. Then he straightened and said, "Yes, you're right. I need to think about your dreams and Westron's chant." He scrunched up his forehead and a faraway look came into his eyes. "The chant. A freshwater ocean," he whispered.

"A crystal-clear river dancing with light," Kelly replied.

Evan shook his head. "We'll never reach the water from here. We're much too late in time."

"The portal." Kelly looked downriver. "We must reach the portal."

"Let's go," Evan encouraged her.

Kelly followed a path along the river, with her grandfather right behind her.

They reached the bend in the river. "Can you feel where the portal is?" he asked.

Kelly shut her eyes. She felt the breath of an icy wind collide with a warm southerly breeze. The wind swirled about them. "It's between the two cedars that overhang the path just in front of us." She opened her eyes. "How far back in time must we go?"

"I think we're going to the birthing of the waters. The source of fresh water for our age."

Cold, pure water washed once again through Kelly's mind. "The glaciers," she whispered in awe.

"Yes," Evan said. Evan took her hand and they stepped through the portal.

Kelly caught her breath; cold shivers blew through her. She realized that she was still holding hands with her grandfather. He released her hand and rubbed his hands together. "Look," he said. They were standing high on a barren ridge overlooking a swift-flowing river, but this river was flowing in the opposite direction. It was moving south. She turned to the north and saw that they were near the edge of a great lake, and this river flowed out from it. "Is that Lake Superior?"

"No. I think we are too far back in time for that. Superior has yet to be born." He looked out across the water. "That, I believe, is ancient Lake Duluth. It's even older, far older than Lake Nipissing. It's an ancestor to our Superior."

The sunlight sent water diamonds scattering over the surface of the lake. Kelly pointed to the northwest. "Grandpa, what is that shining so brightly?"

A smile crept across his face. "I believe that's a retreating glacier. We're at the beginning of a new age." He looked out across the water. "This is a glacial lake, a mighty grand one, and here is an outlet." He gestured down toward the river.

"Glacial water. That's what was in the dream!" Kelly said excitedly. "That's what the dream meant; they need pure water!" She started across the ridge toward the lake.

"No, Kelly! Not to the lake!" Evan shouted after her. But the wind had risen, and she didn't hear his warning. As she topped the crest of the ridge, the wind roared over her. She stumbled and fell, sliding down the long icy dune to the lake. The wind scoured her face and hands with its abrasive tongue. The blowing ice and sand dug at her eyes, and still she fell.

She hit the frigid water with a shuttering impact, as if a thousand blades of metal were embedding themselves in her flesh. She struggled to the surface of the water, suffocating in its numbing coldness. The waves bounced her like a leaf and sucked her under again. Fighting her way to the surface, she gulped at the air, and another wave rolled her under. The cold darkness pulled at her, and she felt heavy, so heavy. Her lungs ached.

Kelly struggled. As she tried to surface once more, something wound about her waist and jerked her out of the water. The wind and waves dragged at her body, but the strength of the rope held, and she was pulled ashore. She felt arms around her and someone was carrying her. She felt so tired. She struggled to open her eyes. They felt as if they were made of granite and would not open. Then she heard no more.

"She will come around once she is warm." The voice was muffled.

"Thank God you came when you did, Garth. She'd have drowned otherwise."

"Your calling came to me with such urgency that I knew there was great danger."

"We should never have brought her on this quest. She's just a child." Evan's voice shook with anger. Kelly still could not open her eyes, but she knew he was by her side. She tried to speak but couldn't move.

"You were both given the choice." Garth sounded sad.

"You should have prepared us better." Silence filled the air. "We're going home," Evan said at last.

"I am sorry, Evan. You and she were our only hope. We did not know what would befall you, but you are safe in this place out of time. Let her rest. She will awaken soon enough. Then I will see you into your own time and home."

"Good," Evan answered. Kelly could still hear the anger in his voice. Again she tried to speak but found she couldn't.

Garth was saying, "Our time is over. The end was inevitable; we just refused to see it." Sleep tugged at Kelly as Garth continued, "Go to sleep, Evan. You need your rest, too. Let the warmth and peace of the grove comfort you. I will watch Kelly."

Evan awoke to find Kelly and Garth quietly talking. "You must return to your own time," said Garth. "Thankfully you are well and were not injured. You and Evan must go now."

"No! You need our help," Kelly insisted. "We can't go without another try."

Garth shook his head. "I will not endanger your lives again."

Kelly sat before the fire. "It was my own fault. I shouldn't have run across the ridge like that." She twisted her braid between her fingers. "My carelessness shouldn't cause you to die. And it's not just you; it's all the trees. We can't be that selfish."

"If you went on with the quest, you could endanger your life. I did not think it would be so dangerous for you, or I would never have asked for your help."

"You saved my life, and I want the chance to save yours."

Evan's voice interrupted them. "No, Kelly. You're going back to our time."

Kelly turned, surprised at his voice. She came over and sat beside him. "But Grandpa, I want to help."

He held her to him. "You can help by going back. I'm going to stay and try to finish the work. We'll still save them, but I want you safe first." He hugged her tighter. "This is not a place for you."

"You can't go alone." She cried into his shoulder. "I won't let you!"

"I've given my word to help them, and I don't want them to die. But I don't want you to be hurt, either. I want you to be safe. And I'll be fine going alone."

"Evan, thank you for your help and willingness to go on. But I will take you to your time also," Garth said firmly. "It is useless for you to go on alone. You do not know where the portals are, and you would be trapped. It is best to take you both home." They all sat in silence.

"Kelly," Evan said, breaking the gloom. He held Kelly's shoulders. "Aren't you scared to go on?"

She sniffled, but the tears had stopped falling. "Yes, I'm scared. But I want to go. We can't just let them die, Grandpa. It wouldn't be right."

"I couldn't bear to lose you, Kel." He brushed her hair back with his hand.

"But Grandpa, couldn't we give it one more try? I promise I'll stay right with you."

Evan stared into the lantern light. "It's a mighty big risk."

"I'll stick to the pathways, and Garth will come if we need him. Won't you, Garth?"

"I will, of course, come whenever you need me. But this is your decision. I will say no more."

Kelly hugged her Grandpa. "One more chance," she pleaded.

Evan sighed. "The O'Malleys always keep their promises."

They stood overlooking the river. The portal had once more delivered them to the riverbank. The sun shone brightly, sending sparkles of light dancing across the water. Far in the distance, the sun lit up the horizon in a blinding white blaze. "There is the glacier." Evan pointed to the north.

"Should we have gone there for the water?" Kelly asked. She held a bulging water bladder.

Evan laughed, "I don't think I'd want to make the trip across to get it." He took the sack from her. "No. This river water is just fine. Probably better. It should be a lot less silty than direct glacial runoff." He placed a hand on her shoulder. "And it was much easier to dip it out of this river than from the lake. Lead on, young one. The First of the Four is in our hands."

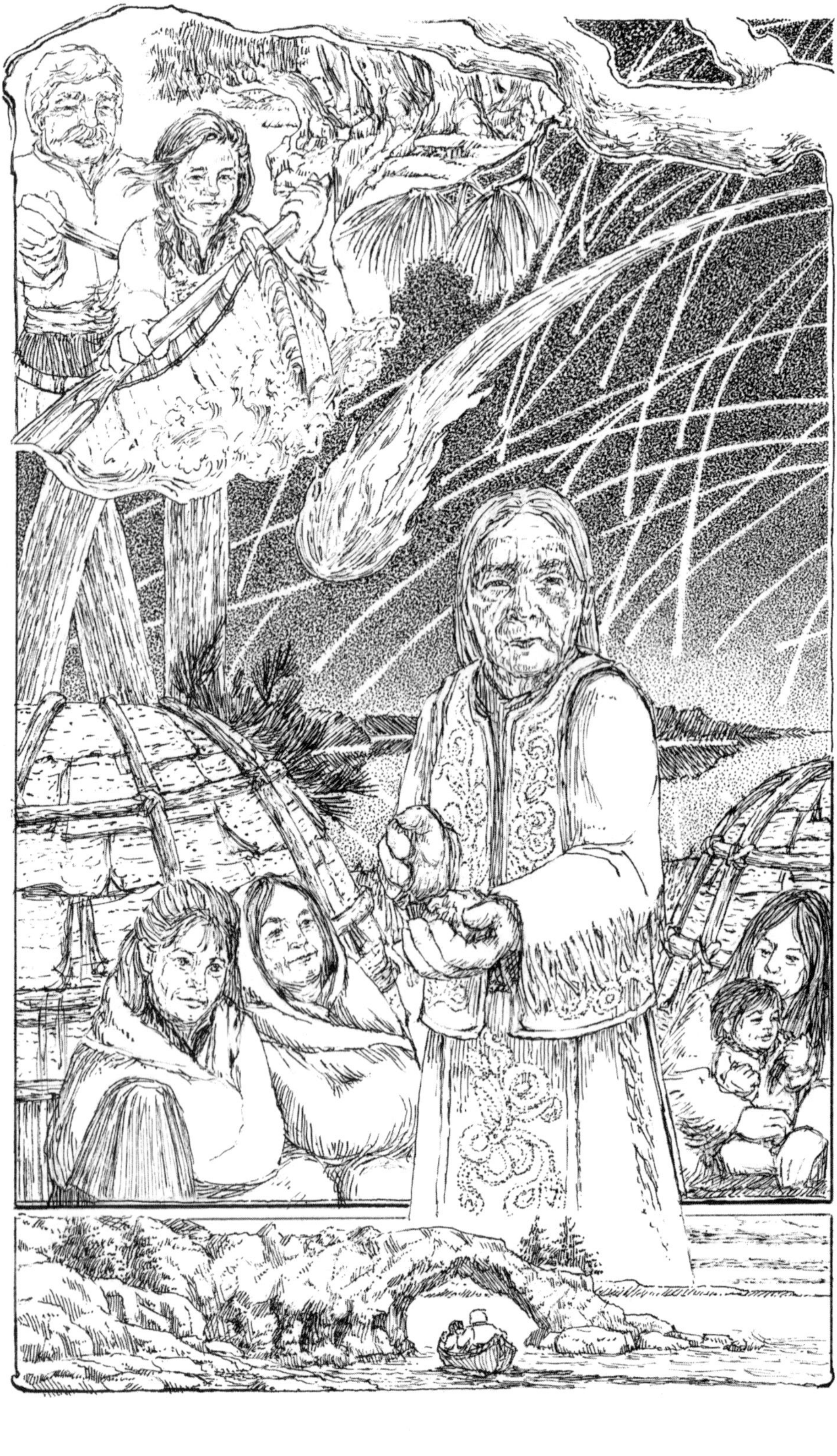

Chapter 6
Copper Country

Several days later they found themselves once again in the company of Garth, walking through the ancient pines. The late evening sun speckled the pine needles with gold. Garth's long robes grazed the edges of the fallen needles as he walked. He seemed more relaxed than when they'd last seen him. *Perhaps,* Kelly thought, *he's just getting more comfortable with moving about again after so many years of confinement.* Garth did appear healthier, and his dark eyes held a spark like a flame when he stood in the sunlight.

"Take care on this journey. You need not travel so far into the past this time. There is no need to see the formation of the pools that you saw in the dreams." He smiled at them. "Be prepared to barter. Good traveling to you!" With a swirl of his cloak, he disappeared.

Evan and Kelly hiked on. "What do you think he means?" Grandpa asked.

"I don't know," Kelly responded. "But remember when I was telling you about the dreams?"

Grandpa nodded.

"Do you think the pool in the dream was a meteor?" The puzzle of the Second of the Four nagged at her. She could see in her mind's eye the fiery ball of light burning into the ground, leaving behind the shiny, coppery pool. "What do you think?" she asked again.

Evan held his hand up. "Patience. I've been puzzling over the chant and your dreams for days, too." He tightened the straps on his pack. "We'll just have to search for it."

They broke camp early the next morning, just after dawn. Feeling the need to move quickly, they hustled to get packed and head out. Kelly followed her grandfather along the lakeshore. In the back of her mind, she heard Garth's warning: *"Do not linger too long in the past."* She didn't think they were lingering, but she didn't want to take chances. What was it they were seeking?

Grandpa interrupted her ruminations. "Kel, what is that over there?" He was pointing to an arched cluster of cedars that stood to the east, away from the lake. Kelly felt an odd pull toward the site.

"It's definitely a portal." Kelly hesitated. A shiver ran through her as thoughts of Lake Nipissing crowded in on her.

"Remember Garth," Grandpa said quietly.

At the mention of Garth's name, a warm breeze swirled about them. Kelly smiled. "Let's go."

As they neared the portal the warm breeze increased in strength and mingled with a fresh wind. They walked through the arch. The wind died down, and Kelly felt her body relaxing. Just beyond the archway, they saw branches bound and set together over a boulder. Looking closer, Kelly found something else. "It's not a boulder. There's something white in there."

Pulling at the branches and sticks, they rapidly uncovered a birch log. "It's just a dead tree, that's all," Kelly said. She stepped back.

Evan continued to tug at the cedar boughs. "I don't think so."

"Why would someone camouflage a log?"

"Come and look at this." His hands ran over the birch bark, then along the side, flipping it over. "A birch bark canoe!" He inspected the seams. "A real birch bark canoe! Someone must have cached it here recently because the seams are still pitchy." He checked the ribs. "No cracks. It looks seaworthy to me." He lifted the bow. "Kel, come and help me pick this up."

He turned to look at her. "Grandpa," she said. She was staring at him in amazement. "Grandpa," she said again, and her tongue felt funny as it rolled over the word. "Is that really you?"

Evan looked equally surprised. "It's me all right. How about you?"

They stared at each other for another moment, and then burst into peels of laughter. Evan finally pulled himself together. "You've changed considerably, Kel. The past can certainly alter our appearance dramatically."

She stood before him, her hair woven into one thick black braid that fell to her waist. She was dressed in a long red cotton dress and pale buckskin overshirt decorated with beads. She looked healthy and strong.

"Grandpa, you must be a fur trader." Evan's silvery-white hair hung to his shoulder blades. He wore dark blue trousers and a fine white cotton shirt. A beautiful woolen sash woven in yellow, blue, and red encircled his waist. An elaborately beaded bag hung from his sash.

"Grandpa," she said, rolling the words around in her mouth, "I don't know what language we're speaking, but it doesn't feel like English."

"Ah, *oui, oui, mademoiselle*. I am a voyageur from Quebec!" Evan looked over Kelly's clothing and his own once again. "Yes, I'd say we are here to trade with the

Ojibway." He pointed to her moccasins. "That puckered seam in the leather is one of their distinctive patterns."

Kelly touched the fine beadwork on her shirt. She gestured at the rest of their gear. "If we've been given all of this, don't you think the canoe was meant for us, too?"

Evan rubbed his chin. "Yes, I think so. We must be about to meet people of this time and place." He turned to examine their packs. "Well, we've got some new goods. There are some deerskin bags here full of flour, blankets, corn, and cloth." He rummaged among the parcels. "Yes, Kelly, I think we've come here to do some trading."

She remembered Garth's words: "Be prepared to barter."

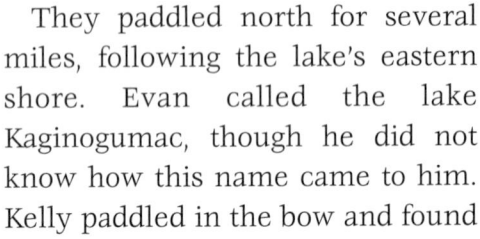

They paddled north for several miles, following the lake's eastern shore. Evan called the lake Kaginogumac, though he did not know how this name came to him. Kelly paddled in the bow and found the ease of paddling to be a welcome relief after days of hiking. The canoe was well-crafted and cut easily through the water.

Evan thought they might be nearing the tip of the lake and began searching the shoreline for an outlet. "Grandpa, on the other shore, I think there's a stream flowing out." They crossed the lake and entered into a small, rapidly moving stream. Sunlight shone through the overhanging maples and cast patterns of green over the water. As they paddled on, the stream grew deeper and wider.

"Watch out for rocks, Kelly. We can't afford to puncture the canoe." She carefully scanned the river, but the boulders were few. The river flowed with the strength of early summer, carrying them high over submerged rocks.

They paddled until late afternoon, when Evan steered them ashore. "I don't want to risk paddling in dim light on an unknown stream, especially with such a fragile craft."

"But I think it was a wonderful way to travel. My feet feel happier already," Kelly said with a laugh.

They camped for the night in a glade of maples and yellow birch. Here and there a huge white pine mingled with the other trees. Before she fell asleep, Kelly rested her hands upon one of the pine trunks and whispered, "If you can speak to Garth, tell him we're fine." No audible response came from the tree, but Kelly thought she could feel it mumbling to itself.

Morning came early. Evan estimated that they were out on the river by 4:30. Kelly couldn't understand how he could possibly know the time. All he would say is, "The sun rises early in the summer, and we're on the river just as the sun is peeking over the crest of the hill." The river ran through a series of narrow canyons. Their steep banks were covered with dense vegetation. They stopped where the stream flowed into a larger river and ate their breakfast of dried meat and berries.

All day long they canoed the winding river. As they paddled along in some of the calmer stretches, Evan would suddenly start singing what he called his traditional chansons like, *"En roulant ma boule roulant, en roulant ma boule."* They would paddle to the rhythm of the song. Sometimes the banks gave way to marsh grass and open meadows, then again they found themselves back in the forest. They began encountering more lowland trees, tamaracks, and spruce.

At times the river narrowed and became rocky. They slowed their pace and paddled carefully through the boulders. Several times, Evan and Kelly waded through the water, pulling the canoe along for fear they would damage it on rocks. In mid-afternoon, they came to a rough stretch of rapids. A kingfisher flew downstream, scolding them with its rattling cry.

They pulled ashore and Evan scouted downriver. "Portage time," he called back to her. They unloaded their gear and carried it around the hazardous water. It took three trips to move all of it to the bottom of the falls. "What do you think of canoeing now?" Evan asked.

She sighed. "Even after portaging all this stuff, it's still better than hiking."

That night they camped on an island of high ground. Kelly fell asleep before the sun reached the horizon. She felt that it hadn't even set when Evan roused her in the morning. *"Alerte! Alerte!* (Get up! Get up!) The sun's almost up, Kel. We've got to go."

After several hours, their river merged with an even larger river. The water here was not as clear, and it seemed reddish to Kelly. There were occasional openings along the riverbanks with trails leading down to the water.

"I think we may be passing through a seasonal village of some kind. There doesn't appear to be anyone here now, though." Evan scanned the bank. "It must not be used this time of year."

"Where do you think we're going, Grandpa? It feels to me like we're getting closer."

"I'm not sure where we're going, but the way is beautiful."

Kelly rested her paddle on the gunwales and closed her

eyes for a moment. "We must follow the river to where it leads." They paddled on.

The river wound through woodlands and then into a large marsh. The marsh was alive with birds. Ducks whisked across the water when they heard the canoe coming. Evan and Kelly startled a heron as it fished the shallows on its stilt-like legs. Mother ducks herded their clusters of ducklings into the reeds ahead of the canoe. They had seen moose and deer occasionally along the river, but they'd never seen as many birds and waterfowl as they did while paddling through the marsh.

The air felt cooler, and a breeze stirred the reeds. They rounded a bend in the river and looked out onto open water. "Ke-che-gum-me," Evan whispered. A birch bark canoe bobbed in the water, blocking their entrance to the lake.

Kelly stared at the canoe and the two people in it, who were calmly watching them. The two strangers picked up their paddles and came directly toward Kelly and Evan. "Be calm," Evan whispered.

"Grandpa," she said, "I'm worried. What if these people don't like strangers?"

"Is that what you feel in your heart?" Evan asked gently.

"No," she admitted. "But that's what my head keeps telling me." She stared at the approaching canoe.

"My heart tells me we'll be safe. Maybe it would be best if we let our hearts guide us through this time and place." Evan paused, "Besides, Garth knows where we are, and nothing's going to harm you or me."

The man in the bow motioned for them to turn and paddle back to the last high ground. When they reached this bit of beach and woodland, they all jumped out of their canoes and pulled them up on shore.

Evan and Kelly turned to face the paddlers. Kelly was surprised to see an older woman and man. They looked much older than Grandpa. Evan bowed to them and Kelly did likewise. The man's white hair was braided, and his breechcloth and leggings were golden brown skins. A thick seam creased the front of his heavy leather moccasins. A string of scarlet berries hung around his neck. The woman was clothed in a pale buckskin dress decorated with the finest quillwork. Her hair also hung in long braids to her waist.

"*Boo-zhoó* (hello)," the man said to them.

"*Boo-zhoó* Grandfather and Grandmother," Evan replied.

They continued in their native language, and Kelly could understand all of their words, just as she'd suddenly been able to speak French a few days previously.

"I was given a vision of your arrival," said the woman. "We have come to meet you and escort you to the island."

Kelly watched nervously, and the old woman turned to her. "Do not be frightened; you are among friends. I can see that you have had visions, too, young one, and this is good."

The man looked them over carefully. Then he nodded his approval. "Let us paddle to the island together and greet our chief." They launched their canoe and led the way. Calm blue water spread out before them like a cape woven from the morning sky and studded with sun-reflecting jewels. The lighter blues of the lake melted into the sky at the far horizon. "Superior," Kelly said quietly. The light breeze riffled the water only slightly. They paddled out on the dark, reddish river water to where it blended into the lake's turquoise blue.

Hugging the shore of a peninsula, they paddled farther out into the lake. Gulls whirled white and cormorants black in the sky against the brightness of the sun. A large bay opened before them. Still farther out, dark green islands dotted the blue of the lake. Hills of green seemed to rise out of the water across the bay. Kelly pointed to the tip of a large island. "That is where we must go. I can feel the quest pulling us there."

"Yes, and that is where they are leading us," Grandpa answered. "Moningwunakauning. Better known to you and me as Madeline Island."

As Evan and Kelly paddled into the vastness of the lake, Kelly felt as if their fragile canoe was growing smaller and less stable. She prayed that the lake would remain still. They both bent over their paddles, and the canoe picked up speed so they could keep close to the elders.

By late afternoon, they were close to the island. Suddenly a dozen canoes were launched from the island, and all of them headed toward Kelly and Evan. They were surrounded. These boats were huge birch bark lake canoes that dwarfed Evan and Kelly's small river canoe. Anywhere from five to twenty men paddled each of these canoes. Kelly realized that the men were warriors, armed with bows, quivers of arrows, and clubs. Her hands shook as she paddled.

Not one of the warriors spoke as their canoes encircled Evan and Kelly. The only sound was that of paddles meeting water. The silence filled Kelly with fright. She gripped her paddle tighter. As they approached the beach, several men came out and grabbed the canoe. They gestured for Evan and Kelly to go ashore. Kelly looked anxiously at her grandfather. He nodded for her to follow him ashore.

Holding up her skirt, Kelly slipped over the edge of the canoe. The knee-deep water instantly numbed her feet and legs, but she kept her balance and followed her grandpa with as much dignity as she could. She didn't want anyone to see how scared she really felt. The elders from the canoe came and stood on either side of Evan and escorted him up the beach.

A man about Evan's age, dressed in finely tooled skins, stood in front of the crowd on shore. Evan walked calmly toward him with his head held high, his white hair almost glowing. The three elders stopped before the chief. Kelly stood behind her grandpa. The chief and Evan looked each other in the eyes. No one spoke, not even the children in the crowd.

Then the chief said to Evan and the two elders, "Come with me. We will talk." He turned and led the way through the crowd, then up the bank toward the wigwams.

Kelly tried to follow, but the older woman turned and motioned for her to stay behind. Kelly looked back toward the lake. Their canoe now lay on the beach surrounded by young men. Her throat felt tight, and an urge to cry welled up inside her. She sat down on the sand and closed her eyes. To calm herself, she thought of Garth. To give herself courage, she thought of the Four of the Past, and the thought of their quest made her smile. The village, the people, and the canoes all faded from her consciousness. Her mind was filled with the quest and Garth. Her grandpa had told her to follow her heart. She felt the pull of the quest. Yes, the strength of this quest was alive here on the island. They had followed the right path. Here they would find the Second of the Four. She looked up. The crowd surrounded her.

A young girl about her own age stood before her. "Come," she said. She took Kelly by the hand and led her through the crowd, down the beach, and away from the people.

"My grandfather's Chief KaKaKee," the girl told Kelly while they ate some roasted fish. They were sitting beside a low-burning fire near the lodges. Kelly translated the chief's name in her mind. He was called "Hawk."

"Where are you from? No one in the village recognizes you."

"We live many days away from the lake, along the banks of a broad river where my grandfather trades," Kelly replied. "My grandfather and I have both had visions and those visions have brought us here to your island."

The girl nodded as she chewed. She brushed back her braids. "You might as well stay with me tonight. Once the elders start to talk about visions and dreams, my grandpa will talk all night, telling stories and asking your grandfather questions." She giggled. "They'll probably still be talking when we get up in the morning."

"Really?" Kelly reached for more fish. "This is good."

"My brother caught it this morning." She stood up. "If you hurry, I'll take you down to the lake to meet him before my mother comes to find us."

When Kelly woke early in the morning, she didn't know where she was. Looking about, she realized she was in a wigwam. Her friend, Médweáckwe, lay sleeping beside her. Kelly smiled to herself as she remembered the meaning of the girl's name: "breath of wind in the trees". *Yes,* she thought, *this is the right place to be.*

Kelly laughed to herself. Médweáckwe had said the old men would stay up all night. Kelly didn't know if grandpa was still up, but the two girls had stayed up late talking and giggling. It felt great to have a friend. She wondered if the elders were getting along just as well.

Médweáckwe's mother and some other women were talking on the other side of the wigwam. Their low voices sounded excited. Kelly strained to hear what they were saying. Slowly, a warm feeling spread through her. They were planning a large feast in honor of her grandfather! Kelly smiled as she snuggled back under the sleeping robes and drifted back to sleep.

Everyone in the village seemed busy with the preparations for the feast. Kelly and Médweáckwe were given chores to do, which kept them busy most of the morning. In the early afternoon, as Kelly climbed the bank from the lake, she ran into her grandfather. He hugged her tightly.

"Kel, everything's going wonderfully. I don't know what Chief KaKaKee has planned, but he says he knows how to help us." He smiled at her. "Are you all right?"

"Oh, Grandpa, I'm doing fine. The chief's granddaughter is like an old friend."

"That's good. The chief's pretty impressive himself." He hugged her again. "It looks as if the Second of the Four may be within our grasp soon."

Kelly didn't see her grandpa again until long after dusk, when the feasting started. He sat with the elders. Kelly stayed nearby with Médweáckwe and her family. The food was delicious. They ate bustards, venison, whitefish, wild rice, corn, and wonderfully sweet drinks. The festivities ran late into the night with singing and dancing. A fog had risen from the lake, and it swirled like a ghostly dancer at the fringes of the firelight.

Chief KaKaKee stood up. The drumming ceased. "It is time for the stories to begin." He motioned for one of the elders to start. The man gave an account of a great elk hunt that happened when he was a young man. Many of the older men and women took turns weaving tales. The fog and firelight softened the air. The storytellers' faces seemed eerie, and even the trees and the ground seemed to float. Fascinated and frightened, Kelly wrapped herself in a blanket and leaned close to Médweáckwe.

After many stories, it was time for Evan to tell of his vision filled with Westron's chanting and of Kelly's vision, and the quest that he and Kelly were embarked upon. "My granddaughter and I have brought gifts to share with you for your kindness and help." He turned to Kelly. "Can you go to the canoe and bring up the gifts?" Kelly nodded and left with Médweáckwe and two other girls.

Evan continued to describe Kelly's vision and the chanting voice he sought to interpret. "This dream was one of four that my granddaughter was given, and this dream has led us here to your village. In this vision, she saw the heat of the sun. The sun spiraled through the sky, and stones of light, rocks of sunlight, exploded from it. Chunks of the sun itself broke away and fell toward the earth, searing into the ground where they fell. The earth smoldered and burned. Then the rains came and quenched the fires. In the pits where the sun had scorched the earth, hard, cold pools had formed that shone like the sun but were as firm as the rocks of the earth." Then Evan sang a portion of the chant he had heard Westron sing in the Council grove.

"My granddaughter and I come seeking to understand this vision and song. The dreams still haunt us both, and it seems to haunt the woodlands where we live."

Evan sat down, and the chief stood. He held his hands out before him and began his tale. "In the times of long ago, almost as distant in time as the stars in the sky are distant from us, the sun sent to this earth a great gift. Father Sun loved the Earth Mother greatly, and desired to send her a gift of beauty to show how strongly he loved her.

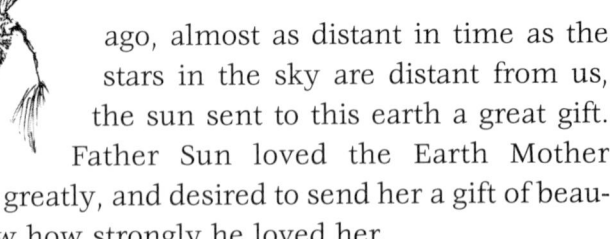

"At this time the earth was still new and not quite done with its growing. The earth stretched and yawned like a young child. Very few people lived on the earth, but there were some who lived along the shores and on the islands of Ke-che-gum-me. They have passed this tale on to us.

"It was in the late summer, when the heat of the sun blazed upon the earth during the day; when the moon did not rise, but the stars shone brightly in the night sky. During these moonless nights, the stars began to cast themselves to the earth. One after another they flung themselves from the skies, until the nights were filled with showers of falling stars. Still, the nights remained bright from the light of stars that hadn't fallen from the sky.

"It is said that the stars fell because of their love for the earth and their wish to send her their light. The earth loved the stars and was pleased with the light they showered down upon her. The sun, hearing of the stars' love for the earth, became jealous and wished to send her a more brilliant gift than that of all the stars combined.

"The next morning, the sun woke from its rest. As the sun rose over the horizon, it began casting spears of flaming light to the earth. These spears burst from the sun and spiraled down. They lit the sky in brilliant patterns of color as they fell. When they reached the earth, they smoked and smoldered. The rains came and drowned out the fires.

"But where the sun's flames had seared the earth where the sun and earth had been joined together, small pools of sunlight remained. These pools were as strong as the rock of the earth, but as bright as the sun. These pockets of sunlight remain about the lands of Ke-che-gum-me as witness to the love of the sun for the earth.

"These sacred pools of sunlight are still to be found along these shores. They are very rare and difficult to find. My granddaughter was called by one of them on the day of the arrival of our guests. She brought this sunlight home to me."

The chief picked up a large bundle wrapped in skins. He removed the skins and took the object in his hands. As he held it out for the others to see, Evan's eyes opened wider. He realized that the chief held a rough ball of pure copper.

"This," KaKaKee said, "we give to our friends who have come from so far to see us." He handed it to Evan, and the two men stood and hugged each other warmly. The chief stepped back and said, "Use this gift wisely."

"We are very grateful to you, and we will use the gift only with wisdom. For you, we leave many sacks of flour, blankets, and other goods. Though this cannot begin to repay you for your kindness, it is all we have." Evan turned to Kelly for the gifts, but she was not there. "Where is my granddaughter?" he asked. "She left long ago with Médweáckwe and several others to fetch our goods from the canoe. Surely they've returned?"

But they hadn't returned from the lake. The chief called to several young men: "Run to the lake and help them carry the bundles!" The men ran off, swallowed by the darkness and fog.

The chief turned to Evan. "Let us sing our songs of celebration." A hush spread through the crowd as the drummers stood and walked to their drums. In the quiet, the drummers raised their sticks in unison, holding them high above their heads. They brought their sticks down toward the skin of the drums. "*Kaaree!*" came a far-off cry, bursting through the stillness. "*Kaaree!*" The war cry of the Ojibway's enemy, the Fox, came again.

A man emerged from the dark trees and fog. "They are gone! The young women have been taken."

They ran to the shore. In the torchlight, the Chief examined the beach. A warrior pointed to a cluster of bushes. "There. That is where they must have waited. They jumped from the bushes and ambushed the women as they walked back from the canoe." Broken baskets and skin bags were strewn on the beach. Evan shook his head. He knew the Fox didn't care for trade goods, not when they could take women. *Garth*, Evan swore to himself, *nothing better happen to those girls.*

Another distant war cry pierced the night.

Chief KaKaKee listened intently. Evan was at his side. "Let us go. You'll paddle with me. The stinking Fox will die!" The chief turned to his warriors. "They are heading back toward the southern shore. Paddle swiftly and in silence. The fog will be our cover." The warriors quickly launched their large lake canoes and pursued the Fox.

Evan paddled in unison with the nine others in the chief's canoe. The vision of Kelly burned in his mind as he quietly muscled his paddle through the water during those long, dark hours. Dawn seeped slowly through the fog with a soft, diffused, golden light. But the thickness of the fog held. The glassy surface of the water parted under the cutting bow of the canoes and rippled away as the blades dipped silently in and back. Every ten minutes they stopped paddling to listen, to hear if they were still going in the right direction.

"*Haa!*" The laughter and talk of the jubilant Fox suddenly rang out through the fog. Mile after mile, the Ojibway silently followed the careless voices of their enemy. Slowly they began to close in on their enemy's small, tippy river canoes.

Suddenly the huge lake canoes burst upon the smaller Fox canoes. The warriors attacked. Evan's canoe along with two others charged into a group of five Fox canoes, upsetting four of them. Knocked overboard, the Fox struggled to right their boats. The warrior in front of Evan reached out and clubbed a Fox as he tried to reach his boat. Cries of anger roared from the Ojibway, who lashed out at the Fox as they tried to escape. Warriors clubbed the floundering men. The Fox were beaten and drowned. The cold, deep water of the lake sucked many down into its depths. Some of the Fox in their smaller river canoes outmaneuvered the large lake canoes and broke away.

"The shore!" the chief yelled. "They're trying to escape!" Several of the small canoes had reached the shore. The chief ordered one of the nearby canoes to pursue the escapees. The Ojibway had assaulted the Fox at a prime location. The shoreline was steep and slick. There would be no escape for the Fox. The warriors were closing in on those on shore as they tried to scramble up the slippery bank. "*Ahhhiii!*" the warriors shouted as they attacked the struggling Fox.

A lone canoe was coming directly toward them. A cry rose up among the warriors. "The women!"

"Granddaughter!" shouted Evan. Kelly and Méd-weáckwe pulled up next to the chief's boat.

"Grandfather!" both girls cried as they scrambled aboard and hugged Evan and the chief. "Thank God you're safe," whispered Evan as he held Kelly.

"Where are the other girls?" the chief asked.

"They're safe on one of our other canoes," Médweáckwe said. "Thank you for coming after us. You saved our lives." She shuddered at the thought of what might have happened.

Both girls were wet and cold. They wrapped themselves in blankets. Kelly shook and tears rolled down her cheeks.

"*Ahhhiii!*" Cries came from a distance up the shore as the last of the Fox stragglers were killed. The water was littered with bodies and debris. The lake canoes began to gather together as the warriors whooped and shouted their victory. The fog lifted, and the newly-risen sun shone brightly on the lake as the canoes started northwestward back to Moningwunakauning.

Days later another dawn set diamonds of rose and purple alight on the surface of the lake. Evan and Kelly were surrounded by their friends as they stood on the high bank above the beach. "We have nothing to replace our trade goods that the Fox have destroyed," Evan said to KaKaKee.

"We need no more trade goods from you, my friend. You and your granddaughter have already bartered with your vision, your courage, and bravery in journeying to our island and in the defeat of the Fox. You must take this rock of copper to finish your vision quest, but it is with great sorrow that we part so soon."

Then the chief turned to Kelly and reached out his hands to her. "And you shall be called my granddaughter. You shall forever be a sister of Médweáckwe." Cheers rose from the crowd. "You will be strong and brave on your journeys that follow, in the great distances that you will travel."

Médweáckwe hugged both Kelly and Evan. The Chief led everyone down the path to the beach below.

Several warriors carried the small canoe into the lake and held it steady as Evan and Kelly waded in and climbed aboard. With a wave of their paddles they headed away from the island.

Evan steered the canoe through the early morning quiet. "The Second of the Four has been found in a chunk of copper," he said.

Kelly gazed toward a distant island. "Yes," she said, "and the portal lies around the far shore of that island."

The two travelers bent over their paddles and made a swift crossing. Kelly looked back as they rounded the edge of the island and caught the last glimpse of Moningwunakauning. "Good-bye Médweáckwe," she whispered. Then she turned and watched the shoreline. "The portal lies ahead through that arched rock." They paddled toward the arch and, reaching it, were gone.

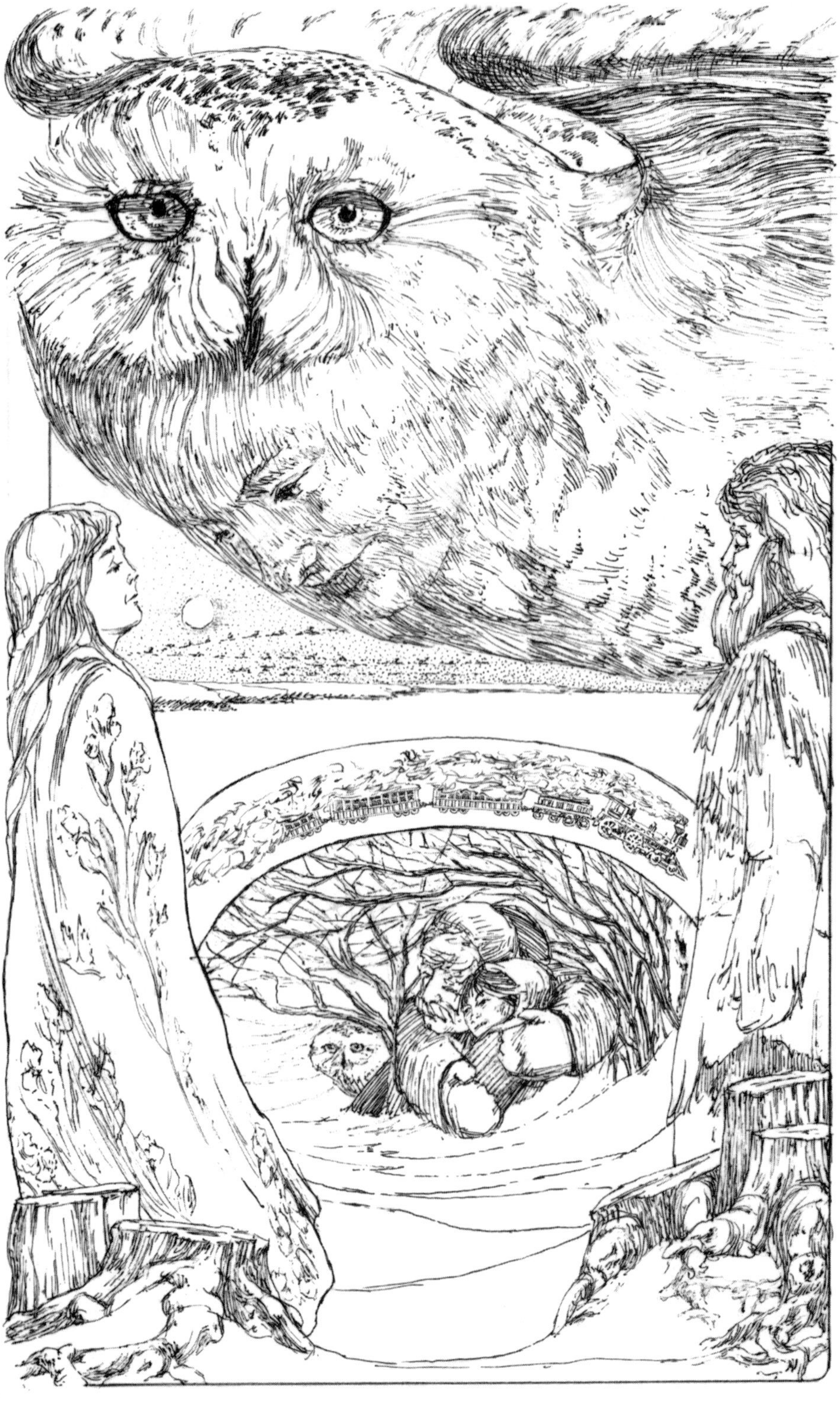

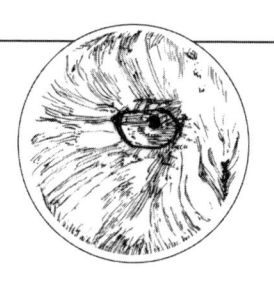

Chapter 7
The Breath of the North

They visited briefly with the Council, but soon Evan and Kelly again found themselves whisked through a time portal into a bitter winter somewhere in the past. For several days they tramped around, seeking a trail that might lead them to the third of their quests, but they could not seem to find a way. None of the routes felt right, and with the continued snowfall, getting around in the woods was becoming increasingly difficult. They decided to make themselves a base camp and operate out of it.

Two days passed, but still the Third of the Ancient Ones that they had come to seek had not become any clearer.

"Gosh, it's cold." Kelly shivered as she sat bundled in front of the roaring fire.

"I agree," Evan replied. "It's a terrible shock to our bodies to go from June weather into the depths of winter." He wrapped his blanket tighter around his shoulders. "I sure hope your grandmother is doing all right."

"She's probably just fine, and it's summer at home! At least the snow's stopped falling here." They huddled by their campfire, beneath a cluster of tall spruce trees. The trees spread their branches out like a large umbrella to shelter them from the snow. The edge of a small canvas tent pegged with wooden stakes poked through the snowdrifts just behind the fire.

"Kel, I know it doesn't feel like we're accomplishing too much sitting here. There's got to be more to this journey than freezing. Something's here that is needed, but I'm just not sure what it is."

Kelly hesitated before she spoke. "Something is happening. At least, I think something's going on."

"What do you mean?"

"I have this strange feeling that we're being watched. Not a scary weird feeling. It just seems that eyes have been watching us, curious eyes following us."

Evan placed another log on the fire. "Who's watching us? Any ideas?"

"I don't know. At first it felt like Garth, but then I knew it wasn't him."

"Try not to worry about it. Whatever it is, and whatever we're supposed to do here, will become clear soon." He rubbed his hands together. "Why don't you try to get some sleep? I'll build up the fire some and bank it before I turn in."

The next day, Evan and Kelly stopped on their hike to rest on a rock outcropping where the wind had scoured the snow away. "Kel, do you feel as if we're being watched again?"

"Someone's eyes have been on us ever since we left camp. And Grandpa," she said, hesitating, "This may seem wierd, but I think I can almost hear a voice talking to me."

"That isn't as weird as it sounds." Evan looked carefully around. "I've heard a voice also. But the voice wasn't speaking out loud; it was talking into my head."

Kelly took her mittens off and held her hands up to her face. "It's like I've got headphones on."

"I feel like it's some type of telepathy. Some people can communicate without speaking. Their minds can send thoughts back and forth."

Kelly looked at her grandfather. "If we are 'hearing' someone talking, can they 'hear' our thoughts also?"

"I imagine they could if they wanted to."

She sat up straight. "Maybe if we concentrate on the voice we've been hearing and ask the person to come and talk with us, we could find out some things."

Evan crossed his arms and leaned back against the rock. "It's worth a try. Maybe it will come to us." They sat quietly for some time.

"As you wish," a voice came into their minds.

"It's the voice!" Kelly cried.

"Who are you?" Evan asked.

"I am of the sky. I have no name, but this," the voice said and their minds whirled, and they were gliding over snow on outstretched wings.

"Oh!" Kelly laughed with surprise.

"Your language is very strange; it is hard to see any pictures in your minds. There are many of those un-images," the voice said.

"Un-images?" Kelly asked in wonder.

"I think he means words," Evan said to her.

"Oh, yes, that is what you humans call them. Words. They seem to clutter up your minds."

"I guess that is often true of humans. Let me introduce us. My name is Evan and this is my granddaughter,

Kelly." Into their minds burst the colors of a beautiful sunrise. "I think he is pleased to meet us," Evan said. Then he addressed the voice. "We are very happy to meet you also." Evan turned back to Kelly. "Try to project those pink and purple shades back to him." They both let their minds concentrate on a sunrise and sent it toward the "voice." An image returned to them of a clear blue sky.

"I think I'm beginning to understand this imaging way of thinking. It's really neat," Kelly said.

The voice said, "It will be easier for you if I try to speak the way you do. But my thoughts may come across both in your words and in my, as you call them, images."

"Do you know Garth? Why did you come to help us?" Kelly blurted out.

"Easy, Kel. We need to take this slowly, one question at a time," Evan cautioned.

"I am picking up disturbing colors from the young one. What is wrong? What is this Garth that makes her so upset?"

"Garth is a friend of ours—a great white pine," Evan began. "We have come here to this time to seek help for him and all of the ancient trees."

"I feel this terrible sadness from you. You care very much for this Garth?"

"Oh, yes," Kelly answered. "Very much."

"Are you what they call healers or doctors?"

"No. We just care deeply for the trees. Their lives mean a great deal to us. We want them to live," Evan said.

"You have traveled a great distance to help them. You say that you have come into this time. What does that mean?"

"We come from a time in the future to find help in the past," Evan replied.

Dark, murky colors of a restless ocean penetrated their minds. "I do not understand. How can this be?"

Evan sighed. "It is difficult to explain. The need was so great that the journey into the past had to be undertaken. Through Garth's powers and the portals of passage, we were able to travel through time."

"What is it that you wish to do in this time?"

"We aren't sure why we've been sent here. We were hoping you might be able to help us."

"Why do you think I might help?"

"Because of the dream," Kelly said. "I think you were in the dream."

Evan interrupted her. "You see, Kelly was given a vision of the Four of the Past. The Four that will help save the trees. In the third of those dreams, there was the coldness and beauty of winter and a bird."

"You are sending me an image of a bird. I will show you who I am."

Evan and Kelly thought an image would enter their minds, but they were startled by the call of an owl as it landed on the rock outcrop above them. The bird shone brilliant white in the sun. "A magnificent snowy owl," Evan murmured.

"You're beautiful," Kelly said.

"Thank you. Now let us begin. I may be able to help you," he said. "You may be able to help me also."

"How can we help you?" Kelly asked.

"I do not know that yet. We must talk some more."

Evan stood up. "First, we've got to get back to our camp; daylight's short this time of year, and the sun is nearing the horizon." He wrapped his scarf tighter around his neck.

Into their minds came a burst of yellow shot with orange, one that could only be interpreted as laughter.

"What's so funny?" Kelly demanded.

"You humans, your eyes are so weak you can barely see in the night. Maybe you should use—what are they called—glasses?"

At that Evan and Kelly laughed, too. "I'm afraid they wouldn't help us in the dark," Evan said. "We can see somewhat at night, but we can see much better in the light."

"Maybe we'll have to get those night-vision goggles," Kelly laughed.

Evan and Kelly shouldered their light packs and started across the rock face to the edge of snow. "Will you join us at our camp?" Kelly asked.

The owl flew up off the rock and circled above them. A band of burgundy rippled through Evan and Kelly's minds. The three set off toward camp.

Tendrils of cirrus clouds, tinted with rose, fingered out across the sky from the west. By the time they reached camp, the colors were fading into the night. Kelly had cached a large supply of wood near the fire pit before they left on their hike. "I'm really glad we've got all of this wood collected. You know how I hate to gather wood in the dark," she said.

"It's a good practice, especially in weather like this. We may need all this wood tonight just to keep warm." Evan had the fire sputtering already and had the soup pot tucked in amongst the ashes.

"What do you think of the owl?" Kelly asked as she dug through the food bag.

"I think we've found a source of help. Somehow he must be part of the Third of the Past."

"I think so, too. But I wonder where he's gone off to." She looked around the clearing but could see no sign of the owl. Suddenly he appeared right in front of her, silently gliding in and landing in the opening away from the fire. Kelly could see in the dim light that he clutched something in his talons. His thickly feathered leg and deep yellow claw jerked slightly as he lowered his beak over the limp rabbit and tore into it. Steam rose from the warm meat.

Kelly closed her eyes. *A rabbit scuttled across the snow, dodging in and out of clumps of brush. Out in the open once more, she saw herself descending toward it, talons stretched out.* And then the image faded and Kelly found herself beside the fire once more.

"What's wrong, Kel?" Evan asked, looking at her with concern.

"The owl," she said in a shaky voice. "I, he, I thought. . ." she stumbled over the words. "I guess he showed me how he caught the rabbit. It was as if I were flying, like I was seeing out of his eyes." She swallowed. "I was just surprised."

"And I bet it was exciting, too?" Evan asked with a smile.

"Now it is. It was scary at first." She moved closer to him on the log.

"This telepathy is a powerful tool. We're both going to have to get accustomed to it." He patted her knee. "How about a little soup?"

After dinner, the owl sent another ripple of burgundy to Evan and Kelly. They replied in a similar manner.

"Are there questions you wish to ask me?"

"Where are you from?" Kelly asked quickly.

"It is too difficult in your words." The owl's voice faded, but their minds were filled with images. They were gliding on powerful wings, and the face of the tundra spread below them. In the heat of the sun, the browns of the northern spring blossomed into brilliant color. They swooped low above the ground, talons barely missing the taller flowers. Amongst the dark rocks and the green of swaying grasses bloomed flowers of yellow and orange; patches of pink laurel hugged the ground. The arctic poppy stood on its spindly, hairy stem, its petals turned to catch the sun's rays.

They circled in flight, and the sun seemed to circle with them. Caribou pawed at the lichens, shaking their heads to chase the flies away. Snow geese strutted near their nests, keeping guard. Young musk oxen and their parents fed in the richness of the valleys. Another snowy owl attacked a lemming and carried it away.

The sun began to fade slowly and steadily. Endless sunlight gave way to the twilight. The flowers faded and withered, their seeds dispersed to the wind. A chill swept over the land. The migrating songbirds of autumn flocked together while the honking of the geese shook the air. Then the cold settled in. With the cold came a stillness broken only by the rushing wind ushering winter back to the Arctic.

The images faded and grew darker, until the deepness of night surrounded them. Then a curtain of aurora borealis showered down upon them. Streaks of white and rose and green rippled overhead. Glowing, the sky flickered in its ghostly dance.

The snow whirled and blew; the sun appeared as a distant aura of brightness. Piercing crystals of snow jabbed at their eyes. There was nothing to see but blowing white all around them. The icy breath of the air stabbed at their lungs.

Kelly felt herself shivering, and her grandpa pulled a blanket around her. "I guess it's not so bad here after all," she said.

He did not speak, but held her tight. The owl was gone.

In the morning the owl returned. Their minds were awash with burgundy, and they knew he had arrived.

"I hope you were not upset about the journey I took you on last night," he said.

"Oh, no," Evan replied. "It was fascinating. I've always wanted to visit the Arctic. Perhaps someday, when all this is over, I will be able to come to your home myself."

"I would be honored." He then addressed Kelly. "I did not frighten you with our flight? You seemed to be a bit gray."

"I was a little scared," she admitted. "But I really enjoyed it. The Arctic is so different and beautiful in its own way."

"And dangerous, too. But yes, beautiful. I miss it while I am here." He sent them images of trees, visions of soaring over miles of unbroken forests stretching to the horizon. "This is your world. I do like being here." Sunset colors wound themselves about his words. "But it is difficult sometimes for me. I am used to the open lands." Small jets of gray sprung from his thoughts.

"But why are you here?" Kelly asked.

"I have been called because there is danger."

Evan looked at the owl anxiously. "What kind of danger?"

"It comes from where the sun rises. It comes rapidly." Dark waves of charcoal and black flooded out the sunset colors.

Kelly sent the owl comforting shades of burgundy and blue. "Don't be upset. Maybe we can help you."

The owl calmed down, and the shades of gray retreated into the shadows.

"It is long and difficult to explain." Into their minds sprang an image of a snowy owl. It glided through the air and then began to climb higher and higher. The black flecking on its belly blurred into the glowing white of its wings as it soared. Circling round and round, the owl rode the thermals until its body melted into the sky. It disappeared into the air.

The air was clear and sharp. It felt like the first icy streams of snowmelt that flow down from the highlands in the spring. It sparkled in its clarity. And then the owl rose before them on crystal white wings, its body as clear and sharp as the air. Its eyes were no longer the yellow-gold of the owl, but blue as the sky.

"I am the Sky. I am the Carrier of the Air."

Kelly gasped and felt a strong urge to bow down before the owl. But she held herself back and sent images of the sunset colors to the owl. He enveloped both Kelly and Evan in a flood of burgundy. Then he was perched before them on a log once again.

"As the Carrier of the Air, I can feel it and others in distress. Relatives of your friend Garth have called me." Images of white pines mixed with his words. "And so I am here. But first I flew far to the east." Again, gray and black bands streaked into his words.

"What happened when you flew to the east?" Evan asked gently.

"I will show you what I saw when I flew for days toward the rising sun." Into their minds flooded images of wild, snowbound land. They saw trees and snow-covered meadows with frozen creeks curving through them. Lakes rimmed in ice. Elk feeding along the edge of a cedar swamp. They came to a great body of water so wide that they couldn't see across, its shorelines covered with ice. In the center, the lake's water churned dark and foamy. More forest lay bundled in snow. Then they saw smoke billowing into the sky. The snow had turned dark and sooty beneath it. They could hear the screams of the tall pines as they were cut and crashed down to the forest floor. Piles of dead trees lay near the smoke; they were being cut into smaller pieces and planks.

They flew on toward the sun, and the forests became less. Far to the east, across the horizon, something ran straight and fast. As it ran, it belched out clouds of smoke. A haze of smoke lay over the east, and the rising sun burned through it like a flaming disk of red. Then the swift runner of smoke seemed to turn, looking towards the owl, and it began to run straight and fast to the west. They could feel the confusion of the owl as he circled and turned away.

Evan and Kelly sat wrapped in silence. Finally, the stillness was broken by the owl. "You understand this, then?"

"Yes, we understand your images," Evan answered. He added more wood to the fire. "Did you stop at all on this journey? Did you speak with anyone?"

"Yes, I stopped several times. I visited with the pines to the east. They cannot fly as I do, but they are so tall that they can look over the forest and see what is to come their way. They could foresee their own doom. They could see and feel the trees far away being cut. They called the smoke maker the iron horse, but there was no way to stop it." The owl seemed to be covered in a shawl of gray. " I do not understand all of this. I only know it is painful."

"Let's go and see these trees," Kelly said suddenly.

"It is much too far. It would take many days."

"No," Kelly said. "We can travel through a time portal, and you can come with us."

"It's a good idea, Kel," Grandpa said. "We can at least speak with some of the trees and give them hope."

"Can you help them?" the owl asked.

"We can't save them, but we can try to help them understand."

"Follow us," Kelly said to the owl. "The portal we need is just over the crest of that ridge." When they reached the ridge, she pointed to a cluster of maples that grew close together. "The portal lies within those trees. Just fly into the center as we walk through." She sent a wave of sunset colors toward the owl to reassure him.

They passed through the hollow of the trees.

They found themselves in a stand of beautiful, ancient pines. The air sparkled with colors of burgundy and green, and Kelly felt joy in their welcome. The owl and trees seemed to be conversing, but Kelly couldn't hear the conversation. The communication between the owl and trees was subtler than her imaging with the owl. It was difficult for her to understand their images and symbols.

Then the owl turned to Kelly and Evan. "My friends, I wish to introduce you. This is the grove of Tavin. May I present Evan and Kelly."

Kelly could feel a slight breeze blowing through the boughs. "Greetings." A voice, which sounded deep and ancient, came down to them. "We are pleased to welcome you. The owl tells us that you are here to help Garth."

"Do you know Garth?" Kelly quickly asked.

"We are distant kin. Is he well?"

"In this time, he is fine. But soon he'll be facing the troubles that plague you. The fate of his grove is the same," Evan answered solemnly.

"The owl tells me that you have come through the portals of time, from the future. Why have you come?"

Evan told Tavin what had happened to Garth—how they became friends, and how his father had promised to help the trees. He explained the quest for the Four of the Past that the Council had set before them. Kelly explained that they had found the first two of the Past and were on their third quest.

"Evan, do you really think that the Four of the Past will help us?" Tavin asked.

"I believe that the Four will help, but how I don't understand. The Council must know, but we don't. The Four must help all of us. For you see, in our time, the first decade of the 21st century, our forests need to grow old. They must know their past, their heritage, for what is the present without a link to the past."

The air seemed to fill with streaks of gray, and the trees seemed to moan in the wind. Evan continued. "The Four of the Past will help change all of that and correct this loss. We must have hope for the future. And you should be comforted by the fact that, far in the future, your offspring will again know this land and grow with wisdom."

Evan and Kelly sat on the ground with the owl. A tall figure in reddish skins appeared before them. His dark beard and hair grew long and curly, the beard reaching far down his chest. The sharp angles of his face seemed to be carved beneath his heavy black eyebrows. "I am Tavin, and this," he held out his hand, "is Beah." A woman came to stand beside him.

Beah was wrapped in a reddish cape the same color as

Tavin's skins. The cape hung in folds to the ground. Dark moccasins peeked out from beneath the cape. Her coppery hair hung down her back. Kelly could see as Beah approached them that her cape was embroidered with many tiny plants and flowers. She smiled at them and seated herself next to the owl. "Hello, my friend. I am glad you have come again to see us."

The owl raised his wings slightly and sent out banners of purple. Beah turned to Evan and Kelly. "I am pleased to meet you. If you are friends of Garth, you are most welcome among us."

"We're happy to meet you," Evan said.

"It's great to meet someone who knows Garth," Kelly said. "Yesterday I was beginning to wonder why he'd sent us here. But now that I've met all of you, I'm beginning to understand."

"Garth is special among us," Beah said. "In fact, I just sent him a message that you were visiting us."

"And I came quickly to join you," Garth said.

Kelly and Evan looked up in astonishment to see Garth before them. "Oh, Garth. I'm so glad to see you!" Kelly cried. He came over to her and hugged her.

"I am pleased to see all of you." Then he bowed to the owl. "Ancient Snowy Owl, Carrier of the Sky and Air, I am honored to meet you."

"The pleasure is mine," he replied.

"I am sorry we must meet under such unpleasant circumstances," Garth said.

The owl ruffled his wings in agitation. "I do not understand why this is happening. Why are so many trees being cut? I see no sense in this."

"Perhaps Evan can explain it better than any of us," Garth said.

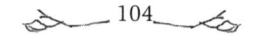

"Men like myself, men such as my grandfather was, are on their way," Evan began. "They are coming to pioneer the land. Some of what they do is acceptable, for many are only trying to survive themselves. They are trying to find a living and support their families. But some of the others act only out of greed. They are an unhappy, selfish lot. They are driven by money and fear." Evan shook his head. "I don't think there is anything we can do to stop them."

"But why?"

"Because they already have a firm grip on the land, and we aren't strong enough to pry the land free. We may not be able to help the present. But we can help the future," he said with determination. He turned to the owl. "Carrier of the Sky and Air, you are the third quest—pure, clean air. We would like to take you from this time back to the Council."

The owl fluttered his wings. "I am willing to join you."

"Garth, is there nothing we can do to prevent the cutting and stop the iron horse from coming farther westward?" Beah asked.

A sad look came over his face. "Until Evan and Kelly came to us, there was nothing we could have done. The ancient race of pines was doomed to extinction." He took her hand. "With their help we now have hope—not for ourselves, but for the future. It is all that we have."

The air was tinged with gray.

"It grows late," Garth said. "Darkness is almost upon us. The three travelers must return to their camp."

Evan and Kelly stood and bowed to Beah and Tavin.

"We shall meet again, my friends," Garth said to Beah and Tavin, and they embraced. "Evan, I will go with you to the portal."

Evan, Kelly, and the owl slipped through the portal and back to their own wintry landscape. The snow was falling heavily as they emerged and began trekking back to their campsite. By the time they reached camp, the wind was blowing the snow in fierce gusts. Five inches of new snow already covered the tent and fire pit.

"It's going to be a rough one tonight," Evan shouted to be heard above the wind. "I'm having trouble getting the fire going."

The owl said, "Evan, I think we should go now!"

The snow was falling faster and thicker. "Yes, you're right." He shouted to Kelly. "Break camp quickly. We've got to find the other portal and get back to the Council."

"Before the storm gets any worse," Kelly added.

"Yes, that, too. I'm afraid that if we try to wait it out, we could be stuck here for several days before it clears again." He was stuffing gear into their packs.

"You are right. This storm will last for days. We must go, and we must go quickly." The owl fluttered his wings.

Ten minutes later, they had their gear packed up, snowshoes strapped on, and they were on the trail to the second portal. Snow swirled around them, falling so rapidly that they could scarcely see. Kelly took the lead, letting her sense of the portal's location guide her. The wind blew in strong gusts, sending shards of icy snow into their faces. Kelly suddenly stopped. "Grandpa, I can't find the way. I can't see," she cried.

Evan put his hand on her arm. "It's all right, Kel, just calm down. It'll be fine." He peered into the blinding snow but could not discern the route.

They all felt the wind, piercing now in its ferocity. "I think the portal is over that way." Kelly's muffled voice came through her scarf. They started out, but the owl called to them, "You are off the trail again." They retraced their steps back to the trail.

The wind struck at them more fiercely than before, driving them back off the trail. They could barely stand up, and they struggled, half-crawling, into the shelter of some cedars. Even the density of the cedar boughs could not hold out much of the wind and snow.

"Grandpa, this is just like those nightmares I had about being lost in a blizzard with the cold pressing down on me," Kelly said. "Where can the portal be?" She moaned. "And what about the owl?"

"I will be fine. Do not worry about me. Remember, I am an arctic bird. But we must find you shelter quickly. There is a cave that I know of not too far from here. Can you follow me there?"

"We'll try," Evan answered. "Let's go, Kel." They crawled out of the brush and tried to stand up, but the wind forced them to lean into the wind. Evan kept Kelly beside him, helping drag her along. They had struggled through a snowdrift and crossed the trail again when Evan realized that the owl, too, was in danger. *If any of us are lost in this storm, the quest will not be completed,* he said to himself.

The wind whined about them as Evan reached clumsily into his jacket and pulled out Garth's packet of seeds. He threw them to the wind, and instantly they were out of time, In-Between Time.

Garth was there, wrapping them in thick blankets, and Kelly realized that they were in the warmth of summer. Garth would close them off from danger. *But where's the owl?* she thought. Into her mind came his voice, "I am right here next to you." He stood on a rock. His voice took on an indignant tone. "I prefer my own means of travel to whatever Evan did to us."

"But we're safe here," Evan answered.

The owl did not reply. Garth said, "Sleep, all of you. We shall talk when you are rested."

"I don't want to have any more of those nightmares." Kelly shivered.

"Sleep," Garth replied. "Your dreams will be those of summer and warmth."

When Kelly woke up, she felt completely saturated with dreams and good feelings. She felt the owl's voice tugging at her, "Wake up, sleepy one. We have work to do."

"What work?" she asked out loud.

The owl replied, "We must finish our journey."

"And bring the owl to the Council," Garth added.

Kelly sat up and stretched. "You can't mean that we've got to go back into that storm," she moaned.

Silently, Garth handed her a bowl of stew and thick slices of bread and cheese.

"Thank you. I'm starving!" Kelly said.

As they ate Garth spoke to them. "The three of you must go back to finish your journey. The storm has passed, and you'll be able to find your way to the portal and then to the Council."

"But Garth," she stuttered. "Why can't we just go to the Council from here?"

"You cannot travel from one In-Between Time to another," Garth answered. "You must go back to the time you were in when you entered this place out of time. Otherwise you'll never find your way back to your own time."

"It is a confusing web. But young one, it is the only way," the owl added.

"How do we know when the storm is over and whether it's safe to go back?" she asked.

"*I* know," Garth said. "I have checked. I will not send you back into any danger."

"Besides," Evan added, "Garth says we've been here for four days."

"Four days?" Kelly sounded incredulous. "I just fell asleep a little while ago."

Garth came and put an arm about her shoulders. "When we come to the In-Between Time, it is a place for rest and rejuvenation. Time passes in its own way, in its own measure."

They found themselves in a fairy-tale world of snow. The drifts were piled halfway up the trunks of the large trees. The saplings and shrubs were completely covered. "This is beautiful," Kelly whispered.

"Yes, it is beautiful, now. But we would never have survived the storm without proper shelter." Evan rubbed his hands together. "I'm glad to be alive, Kel." He smiled at her as he strapped his snowshoes on. "Let's head out."

Purple and orange streamers floated into their minds from the owl as he soared above them. "I guess he's pretty happy, too," Kelly said as she followed her grandpa across the drifting snow.

"Well, this is his kind of weather!"

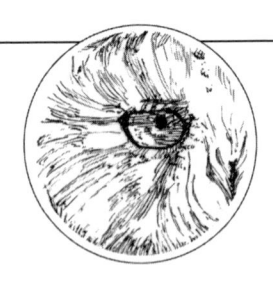

After searching for an hour or more Kelly located the portal. "I think it's buried beneath all of this snow," she said. "But maybe we can still use it by walking over the site."

Evan raised his arm to the owl. "Shall we go?"

With the owl riding on his arm, Evan followed Kelly across the portal. And they were gone.

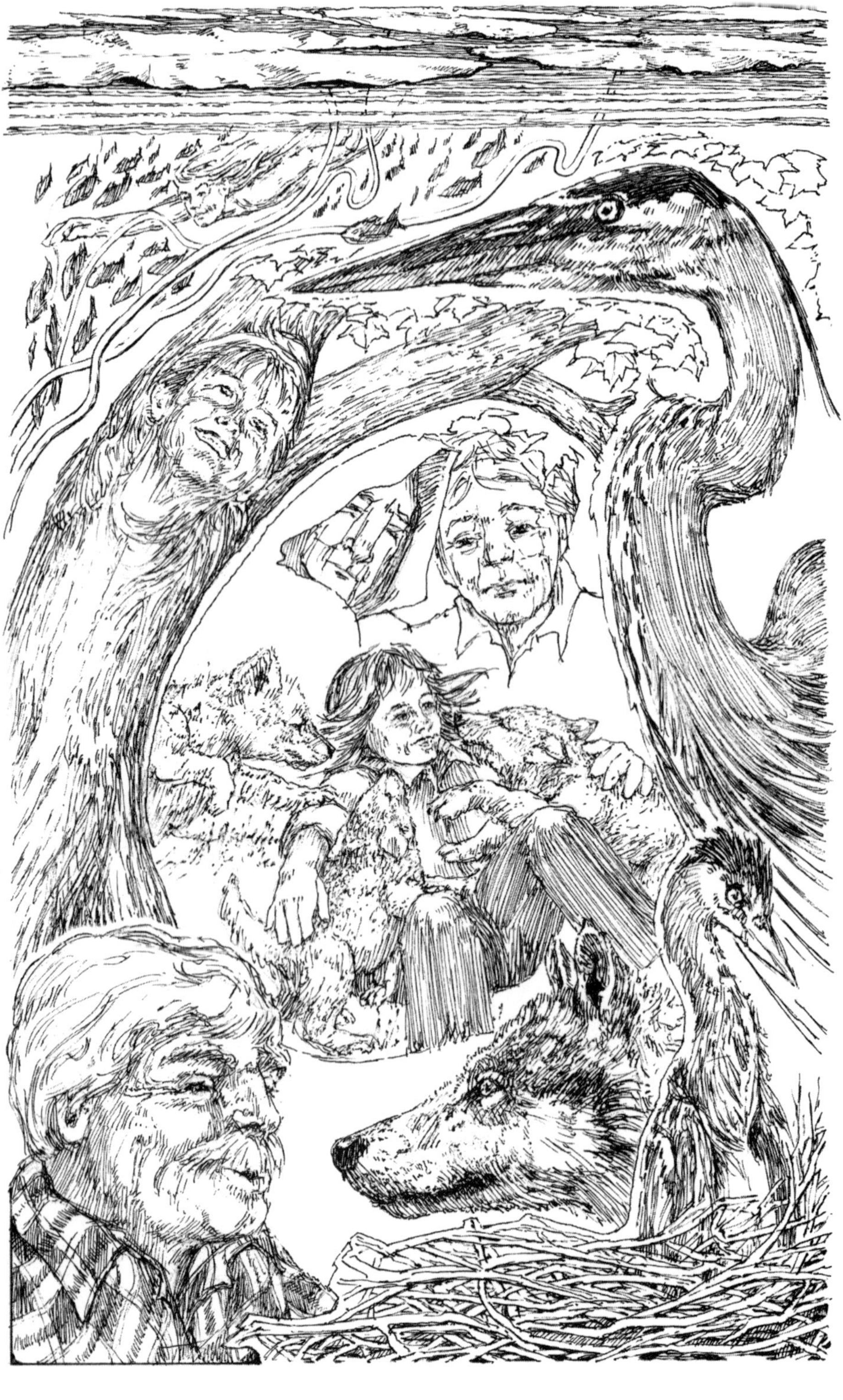

Chapter 8
The Power of Belonging

When they dissolved into the portal, Garth appeared in a filmy haze. "You must go on to the next time," he said. "There lies the Fourth and Final One of the Past that you seek. Good fortune to you." He looked next at the owl and spoke. "However, my friend, you and I have business at the Council."

Kelly and Evan felt a rush of warmth, and the colors of sunset and burgundy flooded through their minds. Then Garth and the owl were gone, and they were standing together on a warm, sunny ridge. Rich green leaves glimmered in the sunlight; a haze of warmth rose from the meadows east of the hill; a buzz of frogs called from the lowlands; a loon cried its wild, laughing call across the lake below the hill.

"Grandpa, I think we've found summer." Kelly smiled brightly.

"I think we deserve it. You know what else? I think there's a beach along the edge of that lake."

"What are we waiting for?" Kelly cried. "Let's go."

They raced down the hill to the lake. Throwing off their shoes and packs on the beach, they jumped in.

Kelly sat on a rock, dangling her feet into the lake. Minnows came close, curious about her; they tried to nibble at her toes. "Stop it," she laughed. "That tickles!" They swam away, startled by her movement.

Kelly lay back and closed her eyes, the warmth of the sun calming her completely. Soon she felt the lake water begin to stream around her. Huge fish surrounded her, their translucent fins flipping powerfully through the water. She felt something soothing her. No voice spoke to her, but she felt deeply relaxed.

The gills of the fish billowed in and out in rhythm. She felt the oxygen filtering in through her own gills. *Minnows?* she thought. *We're all minnows?* Then she felt herself swimming, scurrying along through the water. Her school of fish darted about the rocks and hid amongst the reeds. An enormous fish dashed into the midst of the school, scattering those caught out in the open without the protection of the vegetation. The fish caught one of the minnows and swallowed it whole. Terror rolled through Kelly.

She followed the other minnows and began to eat tiny plants and insects she had never imagined existed. The slight currents of the lake tugged at her body, and Kelly had to concentrate to stay in the reeds and not be pulled out into the lake. They fed peacefully on the algae without further attack.

Crayfish scuttled along the bottom, their crab-claws extended in the dim light. Kelly shuddered at the sight of the pincers, which now seemed so large, snipping at bits of plants.

Suddenly, something sharp pierced the water ahead of her. As it quickly retreated, Kelly saw a crayfish caught in the long, pointed beak of a bird. She swam toward a rock and hid in its shadows. She could see the stalks of the cattails swaying slightly with the current.

"Kelly, Kelly," Evan was calling. Kelly shook herself and looked about. Her feet still dangled in the water over the edge of the rock. The water felt warm on her wrinkled toes, but the air was cooler in the twilight. The first stars were just coming out as the darkness of night spread across the sky, and the shades of blue deepened.

The next morning Kelly dreamed of a great blue heron flying across the lake. Its dusky wings spread wide as it banked in flight. Slowing, it lowered its legs in front of its body and landed in the shallows. When Kelly awoke, she was standing perfectly still, one leg supporting her, the other curled up beneath her. The sand felt firm under her claws, and the water lapped a little way up her leg.

The early morning light continued to brighten the sky as the sun crept above the horizon. She carefully and slowly scanned the shallows.

Her eyes caught a movement in the water. Quickly she jabbed at the shallows with her beak. She brought her head out of the lake, but only water streamed off her beak. Her stilt legs edged stiffly forward, each step slow and meticulous. She watched the water closely. A movement near some lily pads caught her attention. Swiftly her beak sliced through the water. The frog was hers. It struggled as she brought it out of the water. She held it sideways in her beak, and then turned it and swallowed it whole. The frog rippled down her throat. She stalked on along the water's edge.

Kelly hunted until the sun stood well above the horizon and the sunrise colors had faded from the sky. The day held warmth and promise. The morning's stalking had been successful with the catching of a fish, the frog, a dragonfly larva, and a crayfish.

Several quick steps, wings held out, grabbing the wind with sure strokes, and she was in the air. Her wings arched and flexed as she rose. Her heavy neck coiled back to her shoulders, and with her legs dangling out behind, she flew over the lake. Near the center of the lake a pair of adult loons swam low in the water, each carrying a fluffy chick on its back. The yellow and white pond lilies brightly glowed against their green pads; the grasses and cattails grew thicker.

She flew over the marsh and on into wooded wetlands. The air became thick with the cries of herons, and the rookery came into view. Nests crowded closely together hung on the trees. Herons were everywhere: on nests, perched in the branches, in the air. The young stretched their beaks out toward their returning parents, begging for their breakfast. Kelly landed gracefully on the edge of a large nest. Two youngsters immediately badgered her for food. As she turned to them, her grandfather said, "Kel, come back."

She looked at him and shook her head. "I guess I've been dreaming again," she muttered.

"Tell me about your dream."

She told him all about the herons and hunting for breakfast. The early morning stalking and the flight over the lake seemed to interest Evan greatly, so she tried to remember all of the details.

When she finished, he asked her, "Have you had any other experiences like this?"

"Yes. With other animals. Last night with minnows, and since we got here there've been others—a wood duck, a beaver, and a snowshoe hare."

"A minnow? Now that's really interesting. What do you think all this is?"

"The X Files?" Kelly ventured.

Evan laughed. "I'm serious. You know, I haven't told you, but I've been having the same kind of experiences. It's amazing some of the things I've seen and done." He shook his head. "You have no idea what an interesting life a little mouse can lead."

"You were a mouse?" She laughed.

"Well, being a minnow isn't much better," he teased her.

"I guess you're right. What do you think is happening?"

"It must be part of the Fourth of the Past, but I sure don't know how."

"Me either. What's for breakfast? And please don't say frogs and crayfish!"

"Dragonfly soup." He laughed. "Say, how about taking a hike today? Maybe we can find some berries or mushrooms to add some color to our diet."

"A hike sounds great. Let's go this morning before it gets too warm."

By midmorning they were on a trail heading east. "Kel, I'd like to cut across to the escarpment, beyond the blueberry marsh."

"That's fine with me. Isn't that pretty close to one of the portals that we found the other day?" she asked him over her shoulder as they walked along.

He came up closely behind her and said, "Yes it is. There's something special there that I want to share with you."

She stopped so abruptly that Evan ran into her. "Hints?" she asked with a grin.

Evan remained serious. "No hints. None whatsoever. You may as well keep on walking." He nudged her.

She walked a few steps and then said nonchalantly, "So you think I'm really going to like this?"

"Mmmhmm," he answered. "You'll be delighted. But I won't give any hints or clues. Just keep walking. I'll tell you where to go." Kelly gave up and walked on. About twenty minutes later, Evan told her to stop.

"Now I want you to be very calm. Just relax. We're going to cross over this ridge and look down onto a small opening. Don't be afraid."

Kelly looked at him in concern. "But Grandpa, why should I be afraid? Are we going to find the long-lost dragons of Atlantis, or what?"

"Hush," he said. "Remember how you contacted those other animals?" She nodded. "When we climb up here, just let go and try to be calm about what you see. Relax. Be yourself. Reach out to the animals." He led the way up the ridge.

At the crest, Evan hunkered down beneath an old maple tree. Kelly sat down beside him. She looked down into the opening and grinned at what she saw. Five wolf pups played in the dirt in front of an opening in the hillside. They rolled and tumbled, wrestling each other. Then Kelly was among them, wrestling and nipping.

One pup bit her tail and clamped down tightly with his sharp teeth. She yipped at him, but he wouldn't let go until he was attacked by one of the other pups. Kelly turned and jumped on her former attacker, and they rolled through the dust, their tails wagging as they snipped at each other.

One of the pups scurried off. Kelly could see it tugging on something behind some bushes, trying to drag its newfound prize back to the others. Kelly and the rest of the pups raced off toward the bushes to see what the pup was tugging at. They lunged in to tackle their prey. Kelly nipped at its legs while others attacked the tail and neck.

But their prize stood up and stretched, shaking the intruders off. Then he turned and wagged his tail at the pups. They all charged the adult wolf again, biting at his fur and pawing at his mouth. The wolf got down on his front paws, his rump up in the air, and started to play with them. They wrestled and nipped. Kelly joined the others in tugging at his tail or biting his legs. The wolf would bare his teeth as if in fierce combat, then tip one of the pups over with his muzzle and lick its face.

Kelly had hold of the tip of the wolf's tail when he quickly spun around, jarring her loose. She tumbled over and landed in a sprawling heap. The wolf nudged her gently with his paw, and she scrambled up to rejoin the fracas. But one by one, the pups finally staggered off toward the den, Kelly among them, and they settled down to sleep.

The male sniffed at the air and looked around. From out of the den came the pups' mother. Carefully she stepped over the sleeping bundle of young and came up to her mate. They stood facing one another, their tails raised and wagging. They nuzzled their noses into each other's fur. Then they sat down together and looked directly up at Evan and Kelly. Kelly suddenly realized that she had returned to her own body.

"Hello. I see that you have brought your young one to visit us," spoke a voice into her mind. A warm wave rolled over Kelly. "Have you enjoyed your visit here, young one?"

"Yes! And your pups are wonderful."

"Thank you. It's a good season for them. The summer is warm with plenty of food for them to grow strong and healthy before winter comes again."

"Is winter difficult for you?" Evan asked.

"Some are better than others. It depends on how many of us there are and how much food there is." The female looked over at her sleeping brood. "This year there is plenty of food, and all of the young should survive."

The male looked up. "We hunt together. The young and the adults all contribute. This year is one of plenty. Three winters ago, we had only one pup, and even that one could not survive. Our prey was scarce."

"Your pups look healthy and feisty this year," Evan said.

"Yes, but with the news of your quest, I wonder how long we will be able to live as we do. But that is not for us to worry about now," the female said.

"No," her mate agreed. "If there is anything we can do to help you with your work, let us know. The great trees are good companions of ours, and we would like to help them."

"Thank you," Evan replied. "We will help if we can."

The pups woke and began yipping again and tore down the hillside toward their parents. The female wolf lifted her head and howled. Her mate joined in, along with the tiny squealing voices of the pups. Evan motioned to Kelly, and they slipped back down the ridge and started home along the trail.

They sat by the shore of the lake talking. "Grandpa, do you mean we can communicate with all the animals?" Kelly braided strands of grass together as she talked.

"I don't know if we can speak with all of them, but there are many that we can communicate with." He sifted sand through his fingers. "The animals have to be willing to accept us."

"Don't you think that somehow this must be part of what we're searching for?"

"I think so. But I don't know how it will lead us to the Fourth one," he answered.

"Are you worried we won't find it?" She had finished her plaiting and slid the small, woven bracelets onto her arms.

Evan picked up another handful of sand. "If this is part of why we're here, then we should be able to use this ability to communicate in any other time. And I doubt that we can."

Kelly kicked at the sand with her feet. "You mean you don't think we'll be able to 'speak' with the animals and plants when we leave here?"

"I don't know, but it seems to me that this telepathy we're sharing with these creatures won't work in the future. I think they'll be too leery of humans to want to respond to us."

"I hope you're wrong." She sprawled out on the sand, sliding the bracelets over her wrists. "I love it. It's wonderful being with these animals. With some of them, it's as if we become part of them. We breathe and see as they do." She sat upright. "I don't want to leave this behind." She got up and started off down the beach, dropping her bracelets as she ran.

Later that night, Kelly quietly sat in a maple grove. She soon began to grow into one of the trees. Her skin deepened and thickened. She felt the layers building up, one over the other, as the years passed and she grew taller. Her rough skin cracked and expanded. Her bark grew corky and plated. Her roots tunneled through the earth and around the rocks and boulders. They burrowed like small creatures, intertwining with other roots as they grew.

Her branches spread up and outward. They reached toward the sun and wind. They swayed as the autumn winds whirled about, the coolness of the wind refreshing her after the heat of summer. Fists of green leaves were raised to the sun, ready to absorb the sun's warmth when it struck them. She breathed in and out in a slow rhythm.

Evan found her in the morning, sitting beneath a broad sugar maple. He could barely discern a cloaked figure beside the tree. "She is all right," the figure said. "She was troubled, and we shared many thoughts. Let her rest now. I am a friend of Garth's, and I will send her back to you as soon as she is awake." He bowed and disappeared.

"Grandpa, I know I will always be able to reach the pines. Maybe I won't be able to communicate with all of the other creatures and plants. But I know Garth and the pines, and they will always know me no matter what time we're in."

"Yes, we will always be able to speak with you," a deep voice interrupted their talk. Garth strode into the campsite.

"Good to see you, Garth!" Evan smiled warmly.

"Is your quest going well?"

"This is a wonderful place and we're really enjoying ourselves," Kelly answered.

Evan walked over to Garth. "We are working on the quest. We just haven't quite found it yet. But we're very close."

"You're both looking very healthy. I think this time and place is good for you!" Garth laughed. "But, finish up your searching. You need to come home soon, as soon as you can. You can't spend too much more time here or you won't be able to return."

Garth abruptly strode back into the forest. Evan called after him, "We'll see you in a few days!"

After Garth's visit, Kelly and Evan talked more of the quest, and for several days they intensified their searching. They took many long hikes, and spent hours observing animals and watching the lake. But the quiet beauty of the forest slowed their pace. Once again, their days flowed together like only warm summer days can. Swimming and hiking, they sank further into this world of animals and warmth. They soared with the eagles and flitted with the chickadees. They burrowed into the ground with the moles. On silent wings, they flew in the night with the great horned owl. In the early morning mists, they fished with the heron and returned with her to the cacophony of the rookery. They felt strong and comfortable, relaxed in the cycle of life. They returned to visit the wolves and their pups.

One morning, as they watched the loons swimming in the bay, they were startled by Garth's arrival. "Do you know how long you have been here?"

"Garth!" Kelly cried. "I'm so glad you've come back to visit us."

"How long have you been here?" he asked again, his voice distressed.

Kelly shrugged her shoulders. "A week or so, I guess."

Garth turned away from her and spoke to Evan. "Evan, you and Kelly have been here for a month. You must come out. You must come out now."

Evan shook his head. "A month? Are you sure? I don't think it could be more than ten days at the most. We'll have it all figured out in a week or so," he replied calmly.

"No. I have been waiting for you for weeks. We must return to the Council and discuss the Fourth of the Past."

Sadness creased Evan's face. "We haven't found it yet."

"Oh, Garth," Kelly said, taking his hand. "I'm sorry, but we've been enjoying ourselves so much that we haven't really found what we came for. We'll stay here and find it."

"Evan! Kelly!" Another voice broke through the serenity.

"Ann!"

"Grandma, it's so good to see you! How did you find us?"

Ann hugged Kelly, then reached for Evan. She held their hands and looked into their faces. "You must come back now."

"Ann, how did you get here?"

"There is no time," Garth said in a deep voice. "We must leave."

Evan shook his head as if trying to wake himself from a deep slumber. "A month?"

"Evan, hurry," Ann said as she began to throw the camping gear into the backpacks. "We need to do this now. We must leave."

He shook his head again. "Time passes us all too quickly here. But you must be right. Let's get packed."

"But what about the Fourth one of the Past?" asked Kelly.

Garth interrupted her. "Your work here is completed. If you risk staying here any longer, it will be impossible for you to leave. Pack quickly. Let us go before you are caught forever."

Packsack in hand, Kelly looked over the lake once more, as if drinking the scene into her memory. "You will never forget," Garth said quietly to her. She shut her eyes. The loon called, and Garth's cloak spun around her.

"Come. Let us talk before we go to the Council." Garth led them to a knoll, where they sat down. "You feel that you have failed in this journey."

"Yes," Kelly said. "Completely."

"I think not. But in order to be certain, tell me what occurred on this journey into the past."

"It was more like a dream, really," Kelly started. "Now that I'm here with you and Grandma, I can't believe it actually occurred. It felt so real and so alive."

"What felt so good and full of life? Was it the warmth of summer?" Ann asked.

"Yes, but much more than that. I felt warm and alive all over, not just from the sun, but inside, too. We could communicate with the birds and animals, as if we were one of them."

"Garth, what Kelly felt, and what I felt too, was that we belonged," Evan explained. "We were a part of everything that surrounded us. We belonged there just like the deer and the heron. There was a feeling of peace, though death did occur. Animals hunted others out of need. But it was all part of a cycle, like an extended family."

Kelly said, "We weren't visitors looking in from outside."

Garth opened his arms wide to encompass them in his embrace. "Do you not understand? This is what you were to find. The Fourth of the Past is joy in life, finding that sense of belonging and being a part of the whole of life. Kelly, these bracelets that you wove from the grasses of the lake will remind you always of this." He held the bracelets out for her to take.

"Where did you find them? I thought they were lost." She picked them up and slid them over her wrist.

"I did not find them. They came to me, seeking to find you." Smiling, he turned to Ann. "Will you accompany us to the Council? We would be honored to have you join us."

Ann nodded. "I want to see the Council. But more importantly, I don't want to let these two out of my sight for a while."

"Do we have to go to the Council now?" Kelly interrupted. "We have so much to talk about with Grandma and with you."

Garth drew his cloak about his shoulders. "I know you all have much to share, but the Council is waiting, and we must go there first. There will be time for us to talk later."

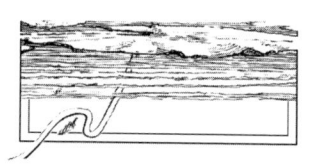

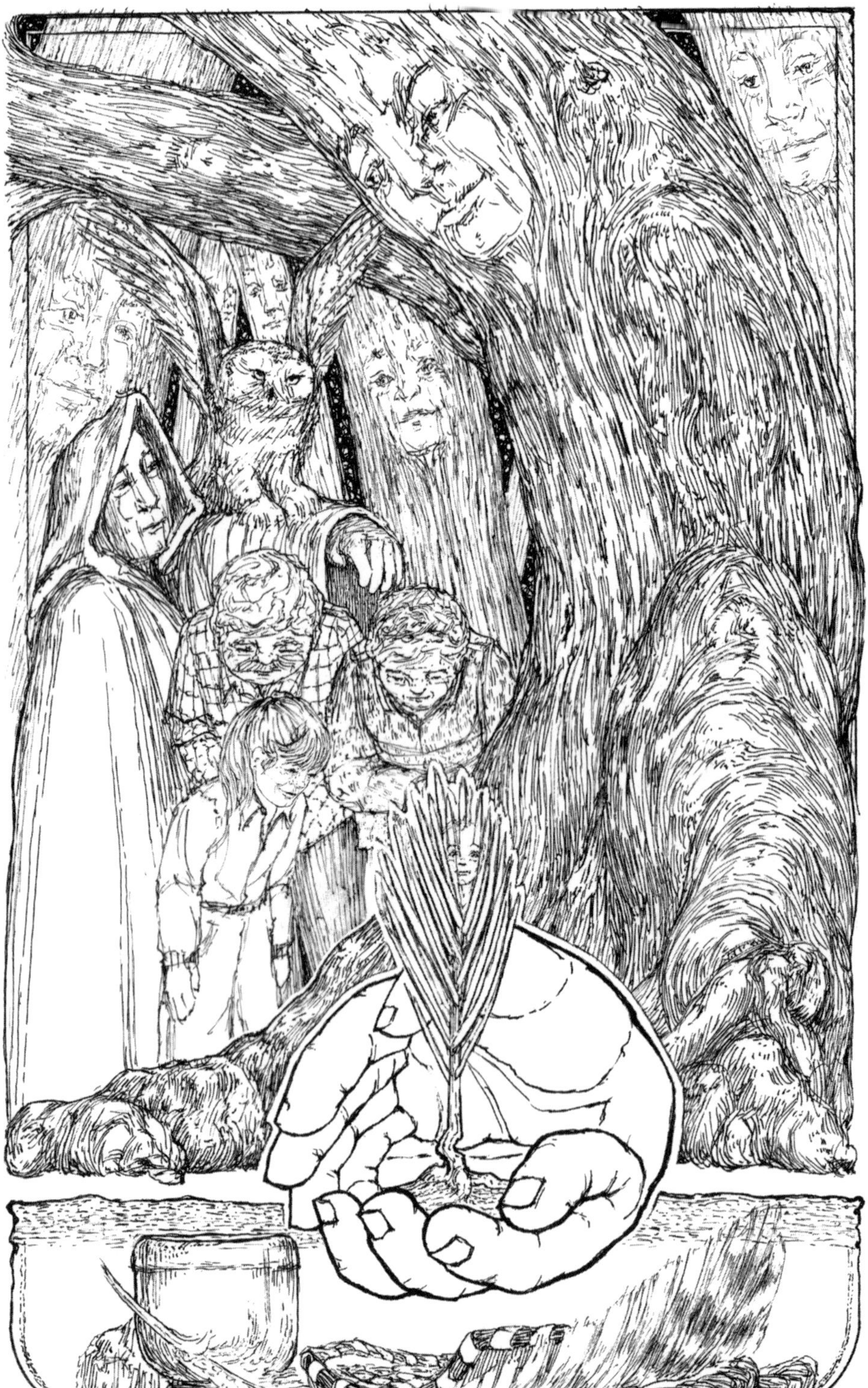

Chapter 9

The Four Come Together

They sat in the midst of the grove, the air warm about them. Kelly saw a star shining brightly through a small gap in the branches high above. She felt comfortable here, as if this grove were another home for her.

Westron spoke. "We warmly welcome Ann O'Malley to the Council. Evan and Kelly O'Malley, we are pleased and delighted to see you on your return. We are happy that you have come back in health and safety. We can never thank you enough for your efforts, for they have brought us new hope for our descendants."

He continued. "You have brought the Four of the Past to the Council to aid us. The Four can now be added to the last of our seeds, which were saved before we were cut. When the logging came so rapidly and thoroughly, we were mostly forgotten. Though a few of us survived and some of our seedlings have grown, our home was destroyed.

"Without the help of the Four, our legacy could not be passed on, nor could our children grow to old age and wisdom. In time, perhaps humans can come to honor who we are and respect us as living beings, and not simply think of us as a source of products."

Garth rose and began. "The First of the Four, pure water, is necessary for all living beings." He took the water sack and filled a crystal glass with it. The water sparkled in the light. Then he set the water sack and glass on the ground before Westron.

Garth stepped back. "The Second of the Four brings us the union of the earth and fire. It represents the many elements that come from soil and the fire and light of the sun." From the folds of his cloak, he brought forth the chunk of copper, lifting it for all to see, then set it before Westron.

"The Third of the Four," he announced extending his left arm. Silently a great white owl landed on his limb as if it were a falcon. "I present the Ancient Snowy Owl of the North, Carrier of the Sky and of the Air."

The owl fluttered its wings slightly. "I am honored to be here. I bring to you air, pure and life-giving." The owl flew from Garth's arm and landed before Westron.

"And last, I bring to you the Fourth and Final One." Garth turned to Evan, Ann, and Kelly and bade them to rise. "They present us with joy in life and oneness with the world. This shall be symbolized by the woven bracelets upon Kelly's wrists." The three bowed to Westron and the Council.

"But they bring us so much more," Garth said.

"Yes," Westron continued. "You, Evan, Ann, and Kelly, are the thread that binds the Four of the Past. Because of your love and caring for us, you risked your lives. Your love will be passed on to our seeds. It brings renewed hope for the future. If you care for the trees that will grow from these seeds, then other people may care also, and this gives us great hope that our wildness and majesty will survive and carry on.

"You have helped bring our full spirit back, and now you will carry us into the forests of your own time. And so we place the Four of the Past in your hands for safekeeping and wise usage. As you are that which binds the Four together, so shall you be the disseminators of our wildness and of the wholeness that ancient forests possess."

They looked at Westron in amazement. "But. . . ." Evan began.

Westron waved him to silence with a gesture of his arm. "There are no 'buts', Evan. You may have thought your quest completed, but really, it has only just begun." He smiled at them. "Only through your work may the cycle of this quest be accomplished." He turned to Garth. "Garth, will you explain the balance of the quest?"

Garth sat facing them. The dark lines and craggy features of his face seemed to have softened since Kelly first spoke with him. She wondered how long ago that had been—perhaps three or six months. He smiled more frequently, and the sternness of his voice had mellowed.

"The quest that still stands before us is of grave importance. Without its completion, the finding of the Four of the Past is all in vain, for the Four can accomplish nothing on their own."

"But," Kelly said, "I thought you would go back in time and give the Four to the last of your seeds, just before you were cut."

"That, unfortunately, would gain us very little. It may help a few seeds, but that is not enough. And those few seedlings, if they succeeded in their growth, would most likely face the same fate as our generation: They would be cut."

"If you don't give the Four to the seeds, what good are they? Isn't that why we had to find them and bring them to you?" Evan asked.

"Evan, of course we're going to give the Four to the seeds, but not in the past. You are going to take the seeds and the Four into the future, into your own time and place. There, the seeds will be planted, and the original bounty of the Four given to each. Only in this way shall they truly grow!"

"Garth, you can't mean that! How in the world would we be able to plant all of those seeds, and where would we plant them?" Evan demanded.

"There are many places where they shall be planted. Safe places where they will be left to grow and live by their own cycle, where no one will cut or harvest them. The first place to start may be your own land. As for planting them all, you will have plenty of help, as you shall see."

"Garth," Ann said, "do you mean that you want us to plant these ancient seeds all across the northlands, where they once grew?"

"Yes. We ask that you plant them in the places where we once lived. Distribute them through the forests and wild lands."

Kelly began to piece together why their travels had been necessary. "We'll be bringing the past into the present."

"Yes," Ann agreed. "Instead of planting apple trees and cultivated crops, we'll be planting wildness!"

Evan smiled at her as he, too, felt the relief of understanding come upon him. "You know, I think you're right. There are lots of wild areas for us to visit, in state and national forests, and on private lands. We need to restore places that will be free of the chainsaw and ax."

"Trees are essential," Ann said. "The earth breathes through the forests but breathes more deeply in old forests. The more seeds we can plant and the longer they can grow, the better the world will be."

Evan hugged Ann and Kelly. "We have much to do."

"Thank you for your understanding," Westron said. "When you are ready, Garth will bring the Four and the seeds to you. We are deeply grateful for your help." Westron and all of the Council bowed to them. Evan, Ann, and Kelly returned the gesture.

"Grandma, why did you come into the past with Garth?" Kelly asked as they sat down at the kitchen table. Evan poured them all tall glasses of lemonade.

"Jan and I had just finished up the paperwork for the botanical survey, and our part of the research was completed. I decided I needed something to perk me up, so I went into Kelly's room to get her new Chieftain's CD. That's when I saw an unusual book on her desk. It was leather-bound and looked very old. Naturally, I picked it up. While I was looking at it, I saw a little door standing open on her desk where I'd never seen a door before." She rubbed her forehead. "I had the strangest feeling that I needed to read this book and see what else was behind the door. Suddenly, a wave of worry for you two washed over me. One thing led to another, and I read all of those journals."

"Are you a detective or a botanist?" Evan asked with a smile.

"Well, we must have left that journal out, but I was certain we'd put everything away and closed the door." Kelly shook her head.

"We had put everything away and the door was shut. I double-checked."

"Garth," Kelly said, and they all started to laugh.

"After I read the journals, I went back to Kelly's room and demanded to speak with Garth. He appeared immediately and just about gave me a heart attack! And then instead of reassuring me that you were fine, he told me that you were in big trouble, and he needed my help to bring you back. He said you were on the verge of being caught in time!"

"Did you believe him, Grandma?"

"I didn't hesitate for a moment. I said to Garth, 'Let's go.' And his cloak flew out around me, and the next thing I saw was you two sitting around your campsite as cool and relaxed as could be." She finished her lemonade.

"You probably wondered what kind of danger we were in?" Evan asked.

"No, I knew. I'd just read those journals, and Garth was saying you'd been in this place for the past month. I knew we had to get you out ASAP."

"You don't think you needed a shower, do you?" Evan asked with a grin.

"My shower felt great. As for you, I think I might have left you a little hot water and soap. I think you need it." Kelly laughed. She walked through the living room and into the kitchen. She felt good dressed in her old blue jeans and tank top. Her hair, brushed over her shoulders, felt silky and soft.

Sunlight warmed the kitchen, and the windows were open wide to catch the breeze. Flies buzzed and battered at the screens, trying to get inside. Kelly's bare feet slid over the cool linoleum. "Grandma," she called, "this salad you made for dinner looks great! But the pizza smells delicious."

"A salad and pizza," Grandpa called. "After pemmican, a salad sounds wonderful. I'm heading to the shower." She could hear him climbing the stairs while she rummaged through the cupboards searching for other treats.

Kelly found it hard to believe that time had passed so slowly here while they were gone. Less than a week had passed since they first stepped through the doors with Garth. It seemed like years. Here, it was only the eleventh of June. She had spent weeks out camping and hiking, and she still had most of the summer left! "The summer's just begun," she whispered to herself.

Garth called to her early the next morning, and she went through the portal with him to get the seeds. They returned to her room with two birch bark baskets filled with pine seeds, the water sack, and the chunk of copper. As they stepped into the room, Kelly realized that her woven grass bracelets hung loosely about her wrists. She smiled as she thought of them and of the lake.

"Now, find Evan and Ann. We will make one more trip," Garth said. Kelly ran off to find her grandparents.

Garth was waiting for them when they returned. "Three of the Four are here, but all of us must go together to bring the other into this time." They disappeared through the wall.

"Greetings," the owl called to them. "Ann, I am so delighted to be in your company once again. But I did not think the other three were ever coming to get me."

"We'd never forget you," Kelly said. "You're much too important."

"Well, I hope so. Are you sure this journey will be smooth? Not like the time Evan took us out of the snowstorm and into the In-Between Time?"

Garth laughed. "This journey will be swift and graceful. But I worry how you will cope with living in such a temperate climate."

"Have no fear for me. I am very adaptable. Is it very warm where we are to go?"

"It is summer in the Northwoods, usually warm, but not hot," Evan answered.

"Well, that shall be no problem. Let us go." The owl flew up to Garth and landed on his arm.

A couple of days later, they were planting seeds north of the house. The owl soared above, watching Evan, Ann, and Kelly. As they made a small hole in the ground, Evan flaked off bits of copper while Kelly set a woven bracelet into the hole. Then Ann placed a seed into the depression, and Kelly moistened it with water from the sack as the owl flew overhead.

"I don't understand how this water bag never gets any lighter, and the bracelets on my arms never get any fewer," Kelly said.

"The copper never gets less either," Evan added.

"There is no explaining it," Ann replied, smiling at them.

The owl perched nearby. "Only Garth knows how these things work. And he will not tell us. I asked him, and he only laughed."

"It is enough that it is so. A never-ending supply of treasures should not be questioned." Garth's voice came through the woods, and he laughed.

"Garth, have you come to help us?" Kelly asked with excitement.

"Or spy on us?" the owl asked.

Evan picked up a basket of seeds. "We won't be loafing too much this summer with all your young to be planted! And by the way, where's all the help you promised?"

Garth laughed again. "Help will come," he said, and his voice faded into the forest. The air whispered with the swaying pines.

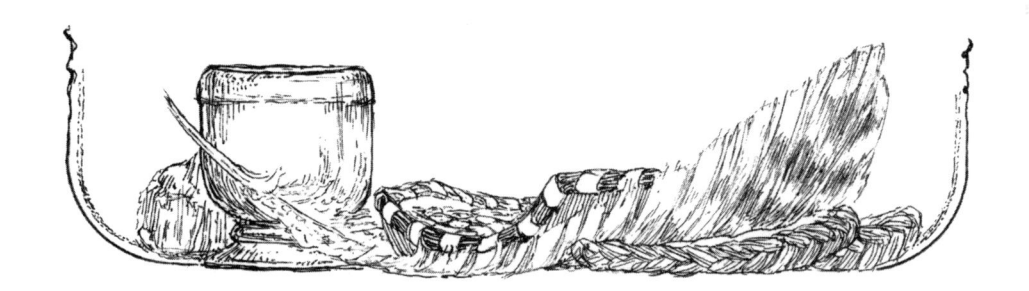

Author's Note

"Planting a tree allows us to think about what we borrow from the future and owe to the past. To sit in the shade of a tree one's ancestors planted is to have inherited space and time and the freedom to walk with them. If you can give such things to grandchildren, you must be accounted rich and wise."

—Peter Steinhart

To walk in an old growth forest is to step back in time, to be in the company of companions who are hundreds of years old.

Garth's home in the northwoods was a pinery, a forest composed mainly of white and red pine trees. In the late 1800s the northwoods of Wisconsin, Michigan, and Minnesota still had about 81 million acres of old growth forests. Of this, about 12 percent, or 9.8 million acres, was pinery. Today, less than one-half of one percent, about 50,000 acres, of this original old growth pinery remains.

There are many natural disturbances to the growth of a forest, like windstorms, insects, disease, and fire. These disturbances cause forests to have trees of different ages, and age diversity is one key to healthy forest ecosystems. But with only one-half of one percent of our original pine forests remaining, we've both cut, and now usually manage, forests to the exclusion of old-growth trees. If some of these forests were released from management, these forests could return to living as a natural, wild community, and more of the trees could grow to their full age.

There are many areas where the pines once grew and, with some help, could grow again. Picture the beauty and strength of those ancient pine forests growing from the seeds you plant. The essence of old growth is alive in every pine seed.

If you wish to help Garth, Kelly, and her grandpa and grandma, we've enclosed a small packet of seeds collected from white pine trees growing in the Great Lakes states. You will find the seeds in an envelope inside the back cover of this book. Plant the seeds by following the directions on page 143, and nurture the seedlings. You will have brought to life a tree that may grow to be hundreds of years old — a tree your great-great-grandchildren may sit beneath, listening to the wind in the boughs.

Sources for Buying Seeds or Seedlings

If you'd like to buy white pine seeds or seedlings, here's a partial list of seed dealers and nurseries who sell seeds and seedlings from the Great Lakes area:

Vans Pines, Inc.
7550 144th Ave.
West Olive, MI 49460
616-399-1620

Great Northern Seed Company
1002 Hamilton Street
Wausau, WI 54401
715-845-7752

Williams Tree Seeds
Rt. 4, Box 275-B
Bemidji, MN 55601
218-751-7957

American Forests' Historic Tree Nursery
8701 Old Kings Road
Jacksonville, FL 32219
800-320-8733
www.historictrees.org

Trees for Tomorrow
P.O. Box 609
Eagle River, WI 54521
800-838-9472
www.treesfortomorrow.com

Organizations

If you wish to learn more about old growth forests, here's a list of some of the many organizations that are involved in trying to protect or restore old growth:

Ancient Forest Explorations and Research
R.R. #4
Powassan, Ontario, Canada
POH 1Z01
705-724-5858
www.ancientforest.org

Earth Island Institute
300 Broadway, Suite 28
San Francisco, CA 94133
415-788-3666
www.earthisland.org/oldgrowth

Eastern Native Tree Society
Robert T. Leverett
52 Fairfield Ave.
Holyoke, MA 01040
www.uark.edu/misc/ents

Eastern Old Growth Clearinghouse
P.O. Box 131
Georgetown, KY 40324
www.old-growth.org

500-Year Forest Foundation
1133 Old Abert Road
Lynchburg, VA 24503
434-384-2324
www.500yearforest.org

Heartwood
P.O. Box 1424
Bloomington, IN 47402
812-337-8898
www.heartwood.org

Minnesota's Native Big Tree Registry
500 Lafayette Road
St. Paul, MN 55155-4040
651-296-6157
www.dnr.state.mn.us

White Pine Society
Ely, MN 55713
www.whitepines.org

American Forests
National Register of Big Trees
P.O. Box 2000
Washington, DC 20013
202-955-4500
www.americanforests.org

Northwoods Wilderness Recovery
P.O. Box 122
Marquette, MI 49855-0122
www.northwoodswild.org

Wisconsin Big Tree Society
P.O. Box 7921
Madison, WI 53707-7921
608-266-2621
www.dnr.state.wi.us

If you want to learn more about replanting forests, check out these web sites:

Forest Conservation Portal
Madison, WI
608-213-9224
www.forests.org

Global ReLeaf Campaign (and other tree planting Campaigns)
1616 P Street NW, Suite 200
Washington, DC 20036
202-518-0044
www.earthday.net

National Arbor Day Foundation
100 Arbor Ave.
Nebraska City, NE 68410
www.arborday.org

Native Forest Network
P.O. Box 8251
Missoula, MT 59807
406-542-7343
www.nativeforest.org

Trees for the Future
P.O. Box 7027
Silver Spring, MD 20907-7027
800-643-0001
www.treesftf.org

About the author:

Mary Burns and her family live in her grandparents' home in northern Wisconsin. Their house will have its 100th anniversary in 2007. Mary, a writer since childhood, writes about natural history in fiction and essays. She is a contributor to *A Place to Which We Belong: Wisconsin Writers on Wisconsin Landscapes* (1998). She is also a professional weaver and works in her studio along the Manitowish River. Much of her artwork is inspired by ancient forests.

About the illustrator:

Peggy Grinvalsky lives in her Lakeland cabin studio and night-walks the forests of northern Wisconsin. Born in 1947 in Torrington, Connecticut, Peggy received her BFA at the University of Kansas, Lawrence, and studied towards her MFA at the University of the Americas, Mexico City. Before settling in the northwoods, she was a medical illustrator in Kansas City, a graphic designer for the BLM in Anchorage, and an art teacher on St. George Island in the Bering Sea. A studio artist for 30 years, her work is in private collections throughout the USA and Europe. A snowboarder and canoeist, Peggy likes to sit on Helen's rock, watch the northern lights, and make new constellations out of the night sky.

About the designer:

Katie Miller is an instructor of graphic design, computer graphics, and photography at Nicolet Area Technical College in Rhinelander, Wisconsin. A professional photographer for 15 years, her nature photographs have been internationally published in magazines, posters, brochures, greeting cards, and calendars. Katie holds an Individualized Master of Arts degree in two-dimensional design and computer graphics from Antioch University in Ohio.

Here's a recipe for how to plant your white pine trees from these seeds:

Since white pines grow in northern climates, and they shed their seeds in the fall, white pine seeds have to undergo winter conditions in order to break their dormancy and germinate (this process is called "stratification"). To simulate winter, take your seeds and soak them in room-temperature water for one day (24 hours). Then place the seeds in moist sand in a clean plastic bag in your refrigerator. The bag should be loosely tied. Keep the seeds in the refrigerator for 60 days before you take them out to plant.

Seeds should be planted immediately after being taken from the refrigerator. If the seeds dry out, dormancy may be triggered, and you will have to go through the same process again. If you want to sow the seeds outside, place the seeds about 1/4-inch deep in an acid, sandy-loam soil. You can add peat moss to the soil to help make it more acidic. Tamp the soil, and lightly mulch the seedbed. Chipmunks and squirrels, among others, will eat the seed, and deer and rabbits will browse the seedlings, so be sure to protect the seedlings when they come up.

If you want to start your seeds indoors, be sure your container is well-drained. A commercial planting soil that has peat moss in it will work well, or simply add peat moss to it (both peat moss and potting soil are available at greenhouses). The moss is important because it holds in the water, and its acidity is important in helping to prevent disease.

Seeds should germinate in about 20 days. Though white pines grow in a variety of moisture conditions in natural forests, for best results, the young seedlings should be watered only when the soil is dry. Seedlings should be 4-12 inches tall before they are transplanted outside. White pines usually grow best in partial sun. Sometimes, in full sun, a pine weevil will kill the leader stem, though not the rest of the tree. Partial shade seems to keep the weevils at bay.

Happy planting!